Of Moose - and - Men

THE SAGA OF TEAGARTIN & CROWFEATHER

- BY -

LOU STANT

COVER ILLUSTRATION BY FR. JEROME SANDERSON.

THE AUTHOR WOULD LIKE TO ACKNOWLEDGE THE CONTRIBUTIONS OF HIS GOOD FRIEND, TIM BALLEW, REGARDING THE STORY'S EARLY CONCEPTUALIZATION AND CHARACTER DEVELOPMENT.

YOU CAN LEARN MORE ABOUT THE AUTHOR AND HIS WORKS ON HIS WEBSITE AT:

WWW.LOUSTANT.COM

PUBLISHED BY HOLON PUBLISHING, A COMMUNITY OF AUTHORS, ARTISTS, BUSINESSES, NON-PROFITS, AND CREATIVE PROFESSIONALS.

WWW.HOLON.CO

Table of Contents

. 1 .

The moose were on high alert. Something in their remote geographic milieu didn't whisper quite right. Being inherently solitary creatures, they nonetheless proceeded through the bottomland, nodding to each other in a spirit of solidarity, having come together out of necessity. They had all experienced it – that nagging feeling that their control was about to be undermined, that anxious awareness of emerging vexation. Several miles to the north something had fallen out of the sky within the past week on an overcast night. Whatever it was the moose could not see, but the sound of it was undeniable, and their keen sense of smell had picked up peculiar odors in the air. Since then they felt threatened, and resorted to strength and safety in numbers. Migrating in a herd was a new experience for these animals, but they felt fortified in doing so. They shuffled onward in a circular pattern that afforded them a modicum of protection, though it wasn't from predators that they felt the need for protection. They feared the unknown.

The disconcerting whisper slowly evolved into a rustle, gaining clarity as it descended from the crest of a tall foothill to their left. The moose ascended the hill, camouflaging themselves in some tall bushes and waiting where they could observe over a long distance what may be approaching. A large bird of prey swooped and screeched above the treetops, and the moose noticed that their collective heart rate had increased. The rustling was intermittently pierced by a repetitive squeek, "....guweeuwee, guweeuwee, guweeuwee..."

And then they saw him. A vast undergrowth of brambles seemed to disappear behind him as he marched toward them pulling his luggage, leaving a strangely civilized enchantment in his wake. He was indeed human, but quite a contrast to the red and black-checkered bumpkins with rifles they saw from time to time. Impeccably dressed in the fine clothing of a cultured gentleman, he seemed utterly unfazed by the wilderness around him.

"...Guweeuwee, guweeuwee..." interjected the wheels under the luggage until he could bear it no longer. He waved a quick halt to his entourage and promptly produced a can of oil with a thin straw spout. Having silenced the impertinence, he continued forward, followed by a sight that the moose would not soon forget. A parade of mammals – deer, coyotes, horses, bears, rodents, bison, wolves, cats, wild dogs, birds - the very picture of subservience and assimilation, carnivore and herbivore, marched side-by-side. They carried and pulled his equipment as if it were a privilege, as if they had been entrapped in a messianic moment, following him at an interval that distinguished their place from his. As much as the proud moose fumed to admit it, Elliot Teagartin's sudden presence was transformative.

· 2 ·

The rusty old bomb had coughed its way from the hills and hollers to the big city. Snaking its way through the broad avenues, stopping and starting, its sooty exhaust exacted consternation from cab drivers at every intersection. Letitia and Daddy Crump stared apprehensively as the buildings became taller. "Lottie," as Daddy referred to her, had never been more frightened in her life, though she could not remember or even imagine a time in her life without fear, never having known the comfort and protection of a mother's arms or breast. The unfolding tragedy of her life began when her mother died giving birth to her only child, an event from which Lottie had never recovered. And now in 1981, 23 years later, she stared out of the car window in awe and panic at an alien landscape, the likes of which she'd previously seen only in magazines. She thought about how much things had changed over the past couple of years since she and Daddy had lost their patch of land to the Savings and Loan and moved into town. They were marginally out of their element in the small town, and now in the big city they might as well be in another universe.

"What was she like, Daddy?" she heard herself ask, as if she were halfway out of her body seeking escape. Daddy's hand was barely on the wheel as he looked for an address.

"Wha...what'd you say, darlin'?" He was somewhat apprehensive as well, but at that point in time he was more inclined toward gleeful expectation. He hadn't the slightest idea what the future held, but he couldn't help but feel that they had been resurrected from the dead, just like Jesus. "It's just amazin' how thangs sometimes turn out..." he thought as he rolled down the window and spat out some tobacco juice onto the pavement. Daddy also thought about how much things had changed, but his thoughts were confined to the past few weeks since Lottie, at his urging, had gone up the holler to the convenience store and spent their last meager resources on some beer and a lotto ticket.

The vehicle lurched while he rounded a corner and slowed down. Lottie looked in horror at a throng of people with cameras and microphones rushing toward them. "This must be the place..." Daddy declared, stopping the car at the curb.

A smartly dressed state official pressed through the sea of journalists to the passenger door.

"Move aside everyone, let 'em through!" He shook Lottie's hand.

"Pleased to meet you, Ms. Crump, I'm John Guhrman, we spoke on the phone yesterday." He held Lottie firmly by the arm and whisked her and Daddy through the crowd toward the revolving doors before them.

Lottie could feel her blood pumping and felt faint, taking momentary comfort in Guhrman's physical assistance. He led them through a lobby and down a corridor through crowds of onlookers who gawked at these new celebrities as if they were at a Hollywood premiere. Lottie felt battered by the loud cacophony of questions and comments directed toward her, which continued unabated until they entered a restricted lounge area, where Guhrman directed them to take a seat. Off to the side stood a door ajar leading to a conference room where a few more officials stood guard. Lottie could hear the sound of a crowd in that room, a threatening white noise that dwarfed the one she had just passed through. The tears welled up and began falling...she couldn't help herself. It was a long-standing coping mechanism that had served her well over the years.

Guhrman didn't seem to notice. "Now Ms. Crump, you remember what we talked about yesterday? This will be a brief press conference. I'll give an opening statement, and you just answer their questions. Just relax and be yourself. I'll keep it to no more than ten minutes." One of the officials at the door motioned at him. "Okay, Ms. Crump, we're ready." He led her and Daddy through the door and onto a stage to a podium, and Lottie could feel the noise in the room decrease, and the tension increase.

The next ten minutes were a blur. Lottie couldn't remember it in sequence, but recalled various disjointed moments. Sequentially speaking, Guhrman began with a two-minute spiel emphasizing the benefits of the lottery to the state, and then introduced Lottie to the crowd. Of course there were the questions, the inevitable absurd intrusions into her privacy, "How does it feel to be a multi-millionaire?" "How do you plan to spend your millions?" etc., etc., etc. She completely blanked when trying to recall her answers, which was just as well, since she assumed that she would be embarrassed by such memories. She vaguely remembered the presentation of the check with the fancy state seal, and an invitation to an upcoming social gala to celebrate the lottery and its new grand winner.

There was one recollection, however, that was distinct. In the back of the room stood an ethereal presence, the Witness - a bearded man in a robe with long sandy brown hair whose head was partially covered in a white hood. It felt to her as if he were somehow in the room, and yet above it. He looked directly into her eyes and appeared to be shedding tears in tandem with her own. Throughout the press conference the presence of this odd stranger softly directed and reassured her, making the experience somehow bearable. When it was over Lottie looked for him, but he had vanished. She described him to the state officials, but they assured her that there was no one fitting that description in the room, that security clearance had been granted only to those on their list.

Daddy Crump was also clueless. "Don't you worry now Lottie, it probly weren't nothin' but nerves... nothin' but nerves..."

· 3 ·

In a field at Wounded Knee, South Dakota, men and women entered the Sundance Circle at sunrise and began their clockwise dance around the sacred cottonwood tree. Simultaneously, the Heyoka, sacred clowns, entered the circle dancing counterclockwise in their ridiculous black and white clothing, attempting to make the other dancers laugh.

It was Piercing Day, the third in the final four days of the "Sundance Ceremony," a Native American ritual lasting 28 days, representative of life and rebirth. Piercing is considered the most sacred part of the Sundance Ceremony, symbolizing the sacrifice that the individual makes for the good of the tribe, and for the honor of Mother Earth and the role of women in the giving of birth. Only a select group of men would be pierced, and these only by invitation. Among the men lying down in anticipation of being pierced by the medicine man was Sam Crowfeather. Two incisions would be cut into his chest, into which pegs would be inserted. Ropes descending from the cottonwood tree would be tied to the pegs, after which he and the other dancers would dance to and back from the tree three times, and then yank back, breaking the skin where the pegs are held. The skin would be cut off and placed at the base of the tree, thus completing the sacrifice.

Leading up to this moment Sam had spent a year in preparation, which included periods of fasting, meditation, purification in sweat lodges, and a "vision quest," an ancient Native American rite of passage in which the participant seeks spiritual guidance and finds his life's purpose. Sam's vision quest, during which he spent several days alone in a remote area of the Northern Wilderness without food, drink, or sleep, had revealed to him that his psyche was divided between two opposites, that of the red man and the white man, and that he must ultimately choose one of the two. Sam was half-Native American, and half-Caucasian, his father having descended from the Oglala Sioux, and his mother, an American of Russian ancestry. It was the influence of his elderly father that had persuaded him to pursue preparation for, and involvement in the Sundance experience, though his aged mother had been supportive as well. Sam's parents had long encouraged him to seek out his destiny in the world, through communion with "The Great Spirit" as his father emphasized, or "God," as his Russian Orthodox mother asserted. Despite his father's death before the ceremony, Sam had strongly felt his presence throughout the 28 days.

As Sam was dancing in the circle following his piercing, he experienced a vision. To the west, he saw his father's face on the horizon, smiling down upon him as he danced back from the tree on his third retreat. Yanking back, Sam fell to the ground as the pegs were ripped from his chest. He felt no pain.

Father Dominic's Mercedes had just been tuned up and given an oil change. It purred gently down the city streets as he journeyed toward a meeting at the Delmonica with his church superiors. He loved that car, and for a brief moment he considered turning around and heading out west on the open highway. He hadn't been in the desert for many years and something in him yearned for solitude. An avid reader, he had been devouring books lately about the Eastern Church and the monks on Mt. Athos, recalling a time in the distant past when his overriding aspiration had been to soar on wings of prayer. What had happened over the years that had led him to settle for a luxury motor vehicle instead?

Gripped in such a pensive state of mind, he was dreading the meeting. During the conference call, he'd discerned that he was being summoned once again to do dirty work. Having a knack for dealing with messy situations, he'd long ago become their go-to guy on matters of intelligence, and he didn't like it. But what could he do? He was a clergyman in a rigid hierarchy, and at that time an alternative such as escaping into the wilderness seemed, alas, unimaginable.

Noting the marquee at the Delmonica, "Welcome Church Bank Officials!" he pulled into the parking garage. As he walked through the casino toward one of the hotel conference rooms he pondered the spiritual state of the Church while observing men in clerical collars pulling the levers on slot machines. The absurd level of worldliness that had crept into the contemporary church depressed him. It had become merely one among several global corporations vying for influence, and resources were dwindling. A sense of urgency in the tone of his superiors had been palpable, but not sufficient to get them to reveal what the meeting was about, not over the phone. But it didn't matter. He'd find out soon enough.

Passing near the hotel bar, something caught his eye. It was a photograph in a large casing on the wall next to the swinging doors leading to the bar. Under the photograph was the message, "Nick & Gil at the Delmonica Taproom, 9pm - midnight. Come hear old jazz standards from the 20's onward mixed with contemporary favorites." In the picture were the two musicians, dressed in their finest. Fr. Dominic was a fan of jazz music, and had even moonlighted as a musician in the past, but that was decades ago. Vocal jazz had become a means by which he could calm his nerves and elude the pressures of being a priest. Perhaps if he managed to catch some free time he could see the show, he found himself thinking, though only half-seriously. These days he generally just stayed at home and listened to records. Caught in another moment of escapism, he felt someone touch him on the shoulder. He turned around and mustered his warmest response. "Oh, hi Father Joe. How are you?"

"Doing well Fr.," came the reply from one of his superiors. "As good as could be expected. I've been at the black jack table. I have mixed feelings about that, but it does relax me. I can't remember the last time I conducted a church service. You on the way to the meeting?"

"Yes I am, and the suspense is killing me!" Fr. Dominic's retort was a lie. The truth was that he would rather not know what the meeting was about, and felt compelled to disguise a certain contempt for his superiors and their way of doing business in the world.

"Well I think you'll find this a bit off the beaten track from what you're used to. No damage control or cover-ups in this one to speak of. I think you'll find it intriguing."

They reached the door of the conference room, and Fr. Dominic excused himself.

"I'll be in momentarily. Just need to pop into the men's room." He went around a corner to the men's room and sat in a stall for a minute, trying to cool down. His resentment had reached a level that surprised even him this time. He sat there and imagined what would happen if his cynicism were to boil over in front of the men who called the shots, those who controlled his life in a spirit contrary to what their supposed callings should have demanded of them. But never mind. It was dangerous to exercise such imagination for very long. After all, he was a priest under obedience in an organization that did not take kindly to dissent, despite scriptural exhortation to the contrary. For the time being he felt as if fate had dealt him no choice but to suck it up, stuff it down, and go with the flow.

Following the usual exchange of pleasantries, the Board Chairman started the meeting. "Gentleman, we appear to be in trouble. The accounts are declining precipitously. We can't help but reach the conclusion that this is due in part to an erosion in the Church's perceived relevance in the world, that is, in the minds of too many Westerners. Church attendance is at an all time low. The question is, what are we going to do about it?"

Fr. Dominic felt his ire rising. "The Church's relevance would have maintained itself, had it only remained faithful to its original mission," he thought, but he dared not say it.

The Chairman continued, "Now Fr. Joe has an interesting idea that I believe has a lot of merit, so I'll yield the floor right now to him." Fr. Dominic's mood shifted. He was mildly surprised and amused, having never figured Fr. Joe for much more than a glorified "yes man." Fr. Joe stood up, paused for a moment, and began.

"I've been studying the past several centuries of Church history. Though several factors could be posited, it seems as if there is one important element in church life that has consistently caused the Church's popularity to spike over the years, that is, those periods of time surrounding the death and canonization of a saint. I suspect, therefore, that this is what we need."

Another voice in the room interrupted in a tone of incredulity. "But who?!?"

Fr. Joe stuck to his guns. "I'm getting to that." He grabbed a stack of collated copies of newspaper articles and began to pass the copies around the room. On the top of each copy was a recent front-page article with a photograph of an individual who had captured the public's imagination more than any celebrity in recent memory. The person in the photograph was none other than Francis Elliot Teagartin.

Fr. Dominic went to see Nick & Gil after all. Given his distraught spirits in the aftermath of the meeting, however, he barely paid attention to the music. Despite his usual cautious approach to being in public, he found himself slowly becoming plastered. In his estimation, his superiors had completely lost their marbles this time. The dispersed newspaper articles had attested to several supposed "miracles" that were allegedly associated with recent sightings of Elliot in the northern hinterlands and other locations. Cited examples included wild animals having been mysteriously tamed, strange forms of supernatural deforestation, various examples of the transformation of tracts of wilderness into organized infrastructure, and so on. Fr. Dominic was convinced that these accounts amounted to no more than sensational journalism, and that his superiors amounted to no more than clerical buffoons.

In reference to the supposedly tamed animals, a discussion had even broken out among the clergymen about how they'd found the St. Francis of Assisi of our age, a "new and improved nature mystic," with more glitz and pizzazz. Part of him wanted to laugh uncontrollably. Another part of him seethed. He had been assigned to find Elliot Teagartin by whatever means were at his disposal, and to establish the veracity of one of the articles which had put forth evidence of Elliot's demise. After all, a saint isn't a saint until he's dead, right?

. 4 .

The Delmonica Taproom was a fancy enough venue, unlike a lot of the dives in which Nick and Gil had to play. The drinks were free to the musicians, which was a double-edged sword to the beleaguered duo. For the Frenchman, Gillian Apollinaire, the wine he consumed took the edge off the stage fright, and steadied his hands to the degree necessary to reinforce his delusion that he just might be more than a second-rate pianist. For his counterpart, the Russian vocalist and actor Nicolai Zagorski, any alcohol held the distinct potential for inviting disaster, by touching off violent behaviors. Being second-generation immigrants, the two had made a concerted effort to retain in themselves the cultural characteristics of their ancestral countries. Both had experienced significant rejection from their immigrant parents for having had the audacity to choose the profession of musician. Additionally, their fates had rendered them the further affront to have been unsuccessful in the eyes of the culture around them, which tended to view success for entertainers purely in terms of "the big time," as a function of fame and fortune. The two felt camaraderie in this shared experience.

It was there, however, that any similarity ended, for the emotional make-up of these two individuals involved only sharp contrast. Nicolai had a superb singing voice and a massive ego. If talent alone was the make-or-break determinant of an artist's career, he could have become one of the all-time greats. In his clearer moments he demonstrated a prodigious talent for musical composition and arrangement, as well as for theatrical production. But Nicolai had been the victim of dramatic mood swings for as long as he could remember. For the past few decades he had trod the fine line between genius and insanity, experiencing poverty, humiliation, and rejection from those with money and influence. Amid the city's artistic community he had the reputation of being so difficult to work with that no one would have anything to do with him.

No one, that is, except Gillian, who hungered for the big time, but had inwardly faced the fact that he couldn't get there without riding the coattails of someone with real talent. Gillian's partnership with Nicolai, however, was not purely opportunistic. Despite all of his punk affectations, French lover bombast, and artistic pretense, Gillian had a soft spot for homeless animals, and for the suffering of his fellow man. Nick and Gil had persevered together scrounging gigs for fifteen years, often depending upon a paltry night's revenue for their next meal. Nicolai's proclivity for manic behavior and gloomy despair had progressed over the years to the point that Gillian's mediocre talent and questionable ability as an accompanist were the least of his concerns. It was Gillian who would listen to him, accommodate him, give him hope in his darkest moments and massage his ego when he found himself ensnared in fits of creative desperation. Most significantly, it was Gillian who would steer him clear of legal authorities through helping him to temper his anti-social behavior. This final function was soon to deteriorate.

Gillian approached the dressing room after the Delmonica gig feeling excited about the prospect of lifting the spirits of his otherwise morose fellow musician. He was accompanied by two women who were "dressed to kill" as they say. Opening the door, he saw Nicolai seated in a slumped position staring at a crumpled newspaper, which he had been carrying around for days. Nick looked up disapprovingly at him and his companions.

Gil was familiar with that look and ignored it. "Hey, bro... I've brought over some 'admirers,' if you catch my drift. Let's head out on the town...c'mon man, it'll do you some good!"

Nick responded quietly but firmly. "Get rid of them."

"Dammit Nick, don't be an ass this time!"

"GET RID OF THEM!!"

Nicolai was about to go into orbit, and Gillian hung his head. "Sorry, girls..." The women left in a huff.

Nick stood and picked the newspaper up off of the end table. "Read this." Gil was in no mood, but Nick persisted. "READ IT!"

"Alright, cool down!" Gil waited until Nick sat down again and began to read. He responded a minute later. "What the hell does this have to do with us?"

Nick lunged out of the chair and grabbed Gil by the collar, slamming him against the wall in a fit of rage, pinning him by the neck. Gil looked into his eyes incredulously.

"...Nick, I can't breathe..."

Nicolai came to his senses, slowly eased his grip and let go. He sat down again.

"I...I'm sorry."

Gil was still in shock. "What is the matter with you, man?"

A minute of silence went by before Nick responded. "We sucked."

Gil rolled his eyes. "Shit, don't start that again...it wasn't that bad, we got some good audience response." This was a pattern that had begun to tire Gil immensely, but the evening couldn't go on until some processing occurred. "You're getting caught up in all that negativity again...I'm tellin' you it wasn't as bad as you're making it, in fact I think it was one of our better recent performances."

Nick began to calm down, and as usual he found himself cautiously taking Gil's words to heart. After another minute the gothic mood resumed as Nick pointed angrily at the newspaper. "I CAN'T STAND IT!"

Gil was disappointed, having thought that he may have successfully changed the subject. "Nick, let's go home, man....you need to chill."

Now it was Nick who was ignoring Gil. "You know that ensemble gig we have comin' up?"

Gil was confused. "Come again?"

"You know...that State Lottery affair with us opening for Frankie and the combo?" Nick didn't give Gil time to respond. "We've been beating our heads against the wall for as long as I can remember, and that piss-ant hillbilly woman just walks into a quickie mart and wins 245 million dollars! Man I've still got some life left in me, I'm not dead yet. We can still get somewhere but we've got to switch gears. It's time for some alternative measures... we've gotta start thinkin' outside the box, man!"

Gil didn't like the look that was washing over his friend's face. Progressive desperation. He'd seen it before. "Man I think you need to go home and get some sleep, you're not makin' sense."

Nick stood up suddenly. "Don't patronize me! I've got a mother already and I don't need another one."

Gil could tell that he would be in it for the long haul. "Okay. I'm sorry... you were leading up to something?" Gil waited for a response.

"Well?"

. *5* .

A few mountain streams converged to form a scenic spring, a "watering hole," if you will. Elliot was famished after a strenuous day with his four-legged apostles and judged that this would be a splendid locale to inhabit, or "make camp," as they would say in the plebian parlance that he so detested. In relatively little time he had worked his magic, and a village was formed. Each of the hundreds in his migratory party knew his or her role, and Elliot hadn't lifted a finger. He relaxed in his easy chair, smoking his pipe and reading the evening paper.

Finding nothing of particular interest in the paper, he set it down and observed the various creatures in his midst engaged in the duties to which he'd appointed them. "I've certainly come a long way," he thought, congratulating himself. But Elliot had been feeling the consequences of the aging process for some time now, and momentarily pondered also how he may somehow tap into the energy displayed by these animals. Being exhausted, he closed his eyes and his thoughts drifted back to a memory from his distant past. He was in his twenties, perhaps 28, when he'd first discovered that he had "a way" with animals. The vivid recollection found him in a habitat of tigers at the Memphis Zoo at feeding time. The mammoth felines were clearly hungry, as they paced back and forth and waited for zoo staff to unlock the cage with red meat for the evening meal. One of the tigers was apparently impatient and lunged at the staffer carrying the meat. Elliot quickly but delicately saw to it that the cage door was latched and slowly approached the roaring beast, which had knocked the staff person to the ground, poised to brutalize him. As the animal looked up at him, Elliot locked eyes with the tiger for a tense moment before the large creature slowly ceased its threatening behavior and walked a few feet away and sat down, having somehow calmed itself through Elliot's influence. The zoo staffer, apparently unharmed, stood up and looked in disbelief toward Elliot before finishing the feeding procedure. As the tension eased, a round of applause broke out among the zoo patrons outside the cage.

Elliot was a prodigy, a charismatic presence not only with men, but other creatures as well. He had been blessed with more than his share of animal magnetism, and had become aware, from a tender age onward, of how he affected living entities when he ventured into their midst. The tendency of men and animals to become quickly fixated upon him was intoxicating to his then-immature ego, and, over the years, fed considerably into the increasingly voracious impulse he had to control his immediate environment. His fascination with the world around him extended beyond his ample gift in the area of economics. Elliot's genius-level I.Q., combined with a profound curiosity regarding the animate nature of reality, prompted him to pursue education not only in the fields of business and economics, but also in psychology, zoology, and wildlife biology. From all of his educational pursuits combined, he had obtained, within a fraction of the time it would take an "average person," four PhDs by his mid-twenties. Animals had always captivated Elliot, and he'd spent a considerable amount of time at city zoos in North America, consulting with staff, and often stealing into animal habitats, with or without the permission of zoo staff. In addition, his wealth enabled him to go on safari in

Africa on numerous occasions.

Elliot's reminiscences were interrupted by one of the bison, who reported to him with an engraved display of menu items on a placard. He looked them over. "I would fancy number seven tonight." The buffalo left with an accommodating snort, and Elliot resumed reading the paper. A spirited marmot scurried up, made a bow, presented Elliot with his aperitif, and scampered away. The odors of a superbly cooked four-course dinner began to fill the air. "Music, please!" Elliot's wish was their command. A general request of this kind always meant Bach, and the dinner smells were soon accompanied in the village aura by the sounds of Baroque bliss, compliments of the bears, who were in charge of entertainment.

Elliot rose to inspect the meal's progress. The raccoons were busy at their culinary duties, blessed as they were with superior fine motor dexterity. Elliot observed as one prepared vichyssoise, and another sautéed truffles in a garlic butter sauce atop a portable camp stove. On another stove a puma delicately poached salmon with champagne and shallots for the entrée. "Coming along well, coming along well..." At this comment Elliot left them to their respective tasks.

As he resumed his relaxed stance, he was reminded of a recent bulletin from the wolves, whose responsibility it was to commandeer the storage wagon. Several items had turned up missing at the previous encampment. A thorough inspection of the premises had failed to retrieve these materials, among which were a set of monogrammed towels, a four-slice toaster, a collection of neckties, a box of butane lighters, and a compact stereo, known in contemporary slang as a "ghetto blaster." Elliot pondered this and intuitively reached the conclusion that there must be a fly in the forested ointment. Somewhere in these heavenward protuberances, otherwise known as "mountains," there was a rebellious spirit at work. It simply galled him to consider the possibility that his efforts at evangelization may have fallen short with respect to one of God's species, and perhaps more than one. He listened and could feel it in the air. Something in this transfigured backdrop didn't whisper quite right.

The high state of alert had given way to a clandestine offensive. The moose were ensconced in a grove of firs a mile and a half downstream. Their territorial sensibilities had been confronted by a foreign presence, to which they had responded by infiltrating Elliot's village mostly at night when detection was less likely. But in their minds this approach was not a hostile one. The moose were as entranced by Elliot as the other animals, but were not as likely to give themselves over wholeheartedly. If they were to be civilized, it would be on their terms.

But how long could the herd hold out? For deep down, the moose knew they were hooked. There were smells carried on the breeze in the evening that made their digestive tracts rumble with an exciting new yearning. The culinary concoctions pilfered from the raccoons utterly delighted their taste buds. The fashion adornments observed on Elliot's brood of cohorts fascinated them with previously unimagined possibilities in relation to keeping warmer in the winter months and looking fetching while doing so. The carpet under them soothed their aching hooves and sent warm sensations throughout their nervous systems. And the music... particularly the Bach and Mozart, enraptured them in a blissful trance-like state in which they felt as if they could reach upward and touch that which was divine. They danced, swayed, and jumped up and down to the music to the point of exhaustion.

On this particular evening, however, the moose were troubled, when, after a period of wrangling, a group consensus was reached with respect to experimenting with the items stolen a fortnight ago. The materials had been kept hidden, but now their collective curiosity had gotten the best of them. A few hours later they were acutely frustrated, wandering about in their surroundings dazed in angst over their inability to fathom the utilization of these items. The presumed clothing draped over their backs with the initials "E.T." looked nothing like the dashing accouterments they'd seen on Elliot's devotees. The long thin pieces of smooth colorful cloth had gotten tangled in their antlers. The multi-colored objects in the cardboard container looked good to eat, but tasted dreadful, and on a few occasions had shot out flames and burned their mouths. The rectangular box with four compartments puzzled and exasperated them, and before they mangled it on a boulder, one of them had been pierced by wire that had been inadvertently extracted from its interior.

The other fancier rectangular box was the great prize among items stolen because of the promise of eliciting the classical music they had so come to love. They were terrorized, however, when, after pushing a certain button, an obnoxiously loud abrasive, dreadful sound assaulted their ears, a pounding, throbbing pulse with a repetitive utterance by some deranged biped, "MOTHERF--!!,... MOTHERF--!!.,...MOTHERF--!!," etc. They prodded it, pounded on it with their hooves, picked it up with their mouths and threw it repetitively onto the ground, until one of them happened to push the button again. The effrontery ceased and their peace was restored, though this particular experience had frightened them to the core. Even more disturbing to consider was the animosity that was beginning to develop among the moose. They found themselves arguing with each other about how to deal with this intrusion into their reality. An innocence had been forfeited over their obsession with Elliot and all that he represented. A cleavage was progressively widening in their communal armor.

· *6* ·

Sam Crowfeather sat in a diner eating eggs. He was reading newspaper clippings and various documents from a dossier. The priest had hired him to find someone, as usual. He and Fr. Dominic went back quite a ways, and on most of those occasions over the years that Sam had been contacted it generally involved matters of some delicacy. He was expected to handle the matter at hand discreetly, but "delicate" isn't an adjective that came to mind in characterizing this one. The priest was always secretive, letting Sam know only so much as to the "why" of the matter, but in the past there had always been clues that revealed a certain "sleaze factor."

In this case, however, he didn't thus far detect anything unseemly. This man seemed lilywhite, at least to the white man's standard. Fr. Dominic had been tight-lipped with respect to the reason he or anyone associated with him would want to find this gentleman, but there was one intriguing fact that he had been directed to establish which involved the issue of mortality. To quote a cliché from a dreadful western he'd seen once upon a time on the silver screen, he was to find Elliot Teagartin, "dead or alive," and preferably dead.

Sam was a self-employed, half-Native American, half-

Caucasian, 56-year-old man, tall, with a rough clean-shaven face and a long black ponytail, who made a living piloting materials to various locations in his Cessna cargo plane, as well as periodically working as a private detective. He had, throughout his life, felt as if there were two forces vying for his consciousness, those of the white man and the red man. Sam considered his plane representative of these two extremes. Being a descendent of Black Elk, the great Oglala Sioux holy man, it was, on the one hand, a metaphor for his desire to "soar like an eagle" in the practice of the mysticism of his ancestors. On the other hand it was the means by which he made a living, often in the employ of the white man.

His fascination with the white man and his achievements on the American continent was as strong a drive in Sam as his spiritual yearning, and it was upon such an accomplished individual that he was now focusing his attention. There were few in the Western World who lacked at least a surface awareness of the persona of Elliot Teagartin. Sam had heard of Elliot many times over the years, and had seen his picture on the cover of such magazines as Fortune, Newsweek, Vanity Fair, and Gentleman's Quarterly, but until now he'd lacked a reason to expand his knowledge of this influential figure beyond a cursory level. Now as he read further, he felt strangely as if he were making up for lost time. He finished one article and began to read a biopic from a declassified FBI file:

> "Francis Elliot Teagartin was born into an affluent family in suburban Boston, and named after the nature mystic St. Francis of Assisi, of whom his mother was a devotee. Mr. Teagartin was reportedly not proud of this, and generally dropped the first name with his signature, while encouraging his friends and acquaintances to refer to him simply as Elliot."

Playing amateur psychologist, Sam pondered this passage, speculating as to whether dropping the first name may have been a result of some kind of conflict between Elliot and his mother. He read further to see if more clues may be offered:

> "A child prodigy in the field of economics, young Elliot handled the family finances from the time he was nine years of age, a responsibility which demonstrated a remarkable inborn ability at investment, a cunning methodology of manipulating the stock market to dramatically increase his parents' already sizable fortune. As a young man in his late teens, Mr. Teagartin came to fully embrace a philosophy of 'Virtuous Consumerism,' a term he himself coined. Such a belief system put forth the notion that through the pursuit of material goods mankind can achieve unity of purpose and find total fulfillment."

Despite his admiration for the white man's achievements, this was a bit much for Sam. "How brazen!" he thought. "Virtuous Consumerism!?... perhaps this guy isn't so lilywhite after all."

> "By his early twenties, Elliot Teagartin was one of the top executives of a multi-national firm, a major shareholder in a number of leading companies from a variety of industries, and an advisor in matters of economics to many high level government officials including the President of the United States. He was soon thereafter to become a sought-after American spokesman, a preeminent upholder and defender of the high standards of Western Culture, a billionaire, and a highly

respected individual among the middle class as well as the elite. He was to enjoy international celebrity status for many years to come."

The more he read, the more suspicious he became. Why would Fr. Dominic and his associates want so desperately to find this guy? Why would they prefer him dead?

"Mr. Teagartin was often on top of media events and seemed to miraculously be present at the location of major happenings before they occurred. He had always somehow been involved in these events and yet remained in the background. His comments on the events were strangely elusive, and were never predictably timed. It often baffled journalists the world over to attempt to determine what exactly these events meant to Mr. Teagartin, though he seemed to consistently pick up the spoils, whatever they were."

Sam was particularly confused at this passage, which hinted at some mystical ability of Elliot's. It somehow seemed to vaguely contradict what he read previously regarding "Virtuous Consumerism." He began to suspect that something dark was at work here, some kind of black magic.

"The mystery surrounding Elliot Teagartin culminated when a small commuter plane, of which he was reportedly one of two passengers, went down in the Northern Wilderness. The plane was owned and operated by Mr. Teagartin, and the identity of the other passenger remains unknown. Mr. Teagartin was last seen boarding the plane with 'a shadowy figure,' who was claimed by tabloids to be connected with the underworld. The wreckage of the plane was found three days after its takeoff in stormy weather. Amid the wreckage were found the remains of a human body charred beyond recognition or identification. Strangely enough, Mr. Teagartin had been in good health throughout his life and had left no medical or dental records behind which might aid in identification. Hence the questions began, "Is Elliot Teagartin dead or alive? If he is alive, where is he? Who was the other passenger on the plane? Whose remains were discovered amid the wreckage? etc." There was a rush by curiosity seekers to find Mr. Teagartin, but to no avail, though sparse reports have surfaced of various sightings in the northern part of the American continent. Despite having found their way into newspaper articles, such reports have been thin on detail and are not considered trustworthy by most reputable publications."

Sam put the dossier away and looked down at his half-empty plate of eggs. He would never be made privy to why the priest had sent him on this mission, though this suddenly seemed unimportant. He now had his own reasons to find Elliot, and would even consider sacrificing the sizable sum Fr. Dominic had been willing to pay. There was something more at stake than money here, though he couldn't claim to have a definite inkling as to what that was. For the time being he would be motivated simply by adventure and curiosity. One thing he felt for certain – he had the wherewithal to locate Elliot Teagartin. He knew these Northern Forests like the back of his hand. And, most significantly, he had wings.

There was a conflagration brewing on the 27th floor of the Tribune, one of two competing news publications in the city. It was taking place in the office of George Cromwell, Editor in Chief. One of his employees was giving him a grilling. "Don't you give a damn that Artie's missing?!?"

George resented the question, but struggled to keep his cool. "Look, I feel as bad about it as everyone else does, but life goes on, and our work here goes on. I'll be damned if I'm gonna let this news organization grind to a screeching halt because one renegade reporter got himself in trouble. If the truth be known, Artie was a pain in the ass. I didn't know where he was half of the time. He had his own ideas and his own agenda, and he was anything but a team player. They had the same problem with him at the Times...that's the lion's share of why he came here in the first place. HELL...HE DIDN'T SHOW UP FOR MOST OF OUR MORNING BRIEFINGS...HAVE YOU FORGOTTEN THAT?!? There aren't many editors who would've put up with his arrogant behavior like I did. I'm sorry he's gone, but frankly, operations around here have been a lot smoother for me without him. As for you, Calen, you need to get back on track and let the police handle this. All you're going to do is muck-up the works!"

Cale fired back an angry retort. "The police aren't doing squat and you know it! They're just as happy he's gone as you are!" George could feel his blood beginning to boil.

"Cale, dammit, in seven short years you've become the best investigative reporter in this city, but you're starting to slip!"

"OH NO... OH NO! DON'T BULLSHIT ME... THE BEST DAMN REPORTER IN THIS CITY, AND PROBABLY THE WHOLE COUNTRY, IS ON THE TRIBUNE'S PAYROLL, AND IT AIN'T ME!! IT'S ARTIE DINSMORE, YOUR ACE IN THE HOLE... SCREW THE DAMN MORNING BRIEFINGS, GEORGE, YOU SHOULD

BE DOING SOMETHING ABOUT THIS OTHER THAN FIDDLE FARTING AROUND, COUNTING YOUR BLESSINGS!!" George was about to blow, and the glass around his office was rattling repeatedly. An audience in the cubicles outside watched to see what would happen next.

"CALE, SO HELP ME GOD, IF YOU SAY ANOTHER WORD, YOU'RE FINISHED!!! NOW GET THE HELL OUT OF MY OFFICE, AND GET BACK TO WORK!!!" Cale got up and stormed out, slamming the door on the way.

. 7 .

Channel after channel of the idiot box threw images into her eyes as if her only duty was to passively ingest without question. It was 4:30 in the morning when Lottie awoke and was unable to get back to sleep. She had dreamed that the Witness came and comforted her, and had vanished in much the same way that he had at the press conference.

Across from her Daddy snored on the plush couch in their hotel suite. Since the presentation of the lottery check days ago, he'd been on one long bender. Liquor bottles were all over the end tables and on the floor, some empty, some half full. Having never stayed at an establishment like this, he didn't understand the concept of daily maid service. He'd run the maids out of the suite on enough occasions that they'd quit coming, and now it stank and was desperately in need of attention. Daddy had been up a few hours ago retching violently in the bathroom, but Lottie assumed that he would be up in the afternoon as usual and would repeat the same drunken pattern. For the first time in his life he was "livin high on the hawg..." as he put it.

She watched him wheeze and snore in violent fits. Turning on the lights, she sadly observed while his eyes opened to half-mast. It occurred to her now why she'd won the lottery. It was for

Daddy. He was having the time of his life, but none of it meant anything to her. Her paranoia and insecurity had only increased in this manic urban environment. She was a misplaced, misbegotten, new-fangled, flavor-of-the-month celebrity, and she only wanted her old life back, to the degree that one would characterize it as a "life."

"Daddy, I want to go home" she heard herself say.

"Turn the damn lights off, darlin', I'm tryin' t' git some shut-eye here!"

She persisted. "I wanna go home, Daddy!"

Daddy sat up. "Lottie honey, now I told you before that we'd go home after the big party." Seeing Lottie hang her head, Daddy continued more emphatically. "Y' gotta go, darlin', you don't wanna be rude to these here people after all they done fer ye, now, do ye??"

She began to cry softly. He wouldn't listen, and she knew that she'd have to suffer through another event.

Daddy got up and stumbled over to the entryway. "Now you go back to bed, darlin'...git yer beauty sleep." He flipped the light switch and turned off the TV, and Lottie sat bewildered once again, enveloped in darkness.

Anastasia sat in the day room sipping coffee, a luxury she had been advised to avoid by staff at her assisted living facility in North Dakota. The caffeine apparently wasn't good for her dementia. Or was it Alzheimer's? She couldn't get a straight answer from the medical professionals. Perhaps even they didn't know. But it was a vicious circle. She wasn't uncooperative by nature, wanting to please those around her responsible for her care, but if she didn't drink the coffee, she'd be in a worse fog all day than if she resisted it. So she indulged in this minor taboo, and felt a sense of anticipation washing over her as she sensed herself becoming more awake and focused. She often knew when a day would have some kind of significance outside of the endless stretch of those that were routine and mundane.

She just knew when something would happen, by a faculty that she couldn't explain, and had long since stopped questioning it or wondering where it came from. It was all part of the mystery that she'd intuitively embraced since her childhood, and had maintained since fleeing Russia with her parents prior to the Revolution in 1917. Her body was aged and ailing, but her mind and spirit were alive and well. Unlike most others she had known over the course of her 94 years, she had sensed the presence of the Holy Spirit in her life and would continue to be faithful throughout her days, despite her current circumstances. Her inner strength had never failed her, and had left her with no doubt that the Spirit was indeed guiding her. She was faithful in all things, except perhaps with regard to always following the advice of her doctors.

Anna, as she was referred to, had a memory that was faltering, but there were things that were still crystal clear. She was remiss in remembering names, people and events from her past, but her prayer life had never been better. The most important things were imprinted within her to such an extent that the dementia, or whatever they wished to call it, was fighting a losing battle in its attempt at thievery. She could recall prayers and liturgical rites with such precision that she even knew when clergymen were subtly violating liturgical tradition during the hours she spent in services at the local Orthodox Church. She had grown too frail to stand throughout the liturgies, but was still drawn into them while sitting, sometimes to the extent that she knew not whether she was in or out of her body.

Yes, something special would happen today, she just knew it. But today wasn't Sunday, or any other significant feast day of the Church. In her mind that could only mean one thing. Her beloved son must be coming for a visit.

A limousine pulled up in front of the bellhops. Daddy stepped out of the lobby with Lottie in tow. He'd given up trying to cheer her up, but had convinced her to attend the gala, motivating her primarily through guilt, as was his custom. Both of them donned ill-fitting formal wear that had been sent to the hotel by John Guhrman. The chauffeur opened the rear passenger door for them and stood at attention.

Daddy smiled his largely toothless grin, marveling at yet another novel experience that he would never have imagined in his wildest dreams only a month ago. "Well now, whaddya thank 'bout that, darlin'? That fancy feller jes opened th' door fer us!"

Lottie felt depressed and sick to her stomach, and wasn't listening. They entered the limousine and sat down next to a wet bar.

"Well, would ya look at that! They got a tavern in this here jalopy... Yeeeeeeeeeeeee haaaaaaaaaw!!!!"

By the time they got through the traffic to the gala Daddy was bombed. Just when she desperately needed his support, Lottie wound up having to support him physically into the ballroom where the huge cocktail party was already well underway. She would not have withstood the embarrassment otherwise to see him staggering around in front of the numerous socialites engaging in the festivities. She delivered him to a seat at one of the tables and went to look for some food and coffee, hoping to sober him up.

Everywhere she walked people stared at her. They smiled, but it didn't feel friendly. She was afraid to stop anywhere and kept walking. She saw musicians in tuxedos across the room departing a stage, having apparently finished their set. After a few minutes she heard a voice through the noise over her shoulder.

"Ms. Crump? Ms. Crump?"

She turned to see John Guhrman with a fashionably dressed woman at his side.

He took a moment to look at the clothes he sent. "Why, you look wonderful, Ms, do you mind if I call you 'Letitia', or 'Lottie', is it?"

She nodded shyly.

"So, where's your father?"

Lottie pointed to the table across the room where Daddy was about to fall out of his chair.

"Oh my..." Guhrman sensed a potential public relations disaster.

Lottie forced speech from her mouth. "He...he needs some food and coffee."

"I'll see what I can do" Guhrman replied. "Liz, can you take care of Ms. Crump for a moment?"

"Of course, dear," his wife responded slyly. She gently took Lottie by the arm and led her through the crowd to a mini-bar. "Will you have anything to drink, or some hors d'oeuvres?"

Lottie shook her head cautiously, feeling profoundly uncomfortable.

"So, have you enjoyed your time in the city?"

Lottie opened her mouth but the words wouldn't come. Her throat loosened. "I...I..." She felt tears well up.

Being an artist, and the frustrated wife of an underpaid civil servant, Liz felt little compassion for Lottie, whom she considered to be an undeserving local-yokel multi-millionaire. "What's the matter dear, don't they talk that much down there in shantytown?"

Lottie looked up suddenly at Liz, stung by the insult. She turned and began to walk away through the crowd swiftly. The walk progressed into a run. She had no idea where she was going, but knew only that she had to get out of that ballroom. Seeing a door by the stage she exited into a hallway, out another door and down some stairs into an alley outside. At that moment the world felt like a cruel heartless place, and she wanted nothing more than to be back at the hotel suite again, enveloped in darkness. She was soon to be granted half of her wish.

· 8 ·

They had been waiting for their chance, and she had fallen into their hands with barely a struggle. Two men grabbed her from behind, and before she knew it she was straitjacketed with duct tape over her mouth. Lottie fainted and went limp as they carried her to a car, put her in the trunk onto an old foam mattress, and sped off into the night. With one hand on the wheel Gil pulled the ski mask off his head with the other and threw it on the dash. He was trembling and sweating profusely. "I will never know why I let you talk me into this!"

Nick was surprisingly calm. "Just shut up and drive."

Gil pulled off into a side street and slammed on the brakes. "You son of a bitch!!!" Gil shook his fist in Nick's face. "YOU TALK ME INTO COMMITING VIOLENT CRIME AND THEN YOU BARK OUT ORDERS? YOU THINK YOU CAN TALK TO ME LIKE THAT? HUH?!?"

Before they knew it there was a rap on the driver's side window. A policeman was shining a flashlight into the car. Gil struggled to regain his composure. He rolled down his window at the cop's behest, and Nick spoke up.

"We're okay now, officer, just lost our cool for a minute."

After checking Gil's license and the car registration, the

patrolman surveyed the insides of the car with his flashlight. "What you got in the back seat here?"

"Just musical instruments, sir," Nick responded.

The policeman looked back at the two musicians and shrugged. These guys seemed harmless enough, despite the scuffle, and it didn't seem worth his trouble to haul them down to the precinct where the jail was overcrowded. "I'm gonna let you guys go. Cool down and take it easy, okay?"

Gil responded this time. "Thank you, officer, sorry for the trouble. We'll be fine." The policeman walked back to the patrol car, and the two kidnappers breathed a sigh of relief. Gil put the car in gear and drove off. Several minutes of silence ensued. Gil got on the freeway ramp and they headed north out of the city. "Tell me again why we did this?" Gil's question was more sarcastic than inquisitive.

Nick looked contritely at his friend. Gil's psychotic fit elicited a rare empathetic response. "I apologize for being such an ass. I can see that this ain't a piece o' cake for you... hell, it isn't easy for me either!" though if Nick were to be honest, he was actually surprised at himself, at how calmly he'd been able to pull off the kidnapping. "Look, those bumpkins are rollin' in the baksheesh, man! Just think about it – 24.5 million dollars! Imagine what we could do with just a fraction of that money. We could make the recording we've always wanted, put a band together and go on tour, get the hell out of that rat-trap and live somewhere decent. Those yokels aren't any more deserving of that money than we are-"

Gil interrupted. "ALRIGHT!... Alright, enough, I don't need to hear it again!" He could sense the depths of yearning in his friend, and had to admit that he shared in the dreams Nick expressed. He was, however, profoundly paranoid about the legal implications of what they'd done, and a bit concerned at how cavalier his friend was in his lack of concern. "Well, I guess it's too late to turn back now. You know we could wind up doing serious time for this, don't you?"

Nick didn't respond, and they continued northward.

Lottie found herself on a beach, witnessing a brilliant sunset, the likes of which she'd never seen. She had been land-locked her entire life until this moment. She looked out on the vastness of the sea and felt its breath, the ebb and flow of its tides. The details of how she ended up on the beach did not concern her. The ocean's breath became her own.

She noticed a man on the beach a ways away, sitting next to a fire, preparing a meal. He was gesturing toward her, gently urging her to come and dine. As she slowly approached, she recognized him. It was the Witness. It occurred to her that she wasn't afraid. She wasn't afraid. She smiled as she sat down across the fire from him. He handed her a cup and a plate of food. The fish and bread were rapturous to her palate, and she ate sumptuously. The wine was unlike any drink that had ever passed her lips. They smiled at each other until she broke the silence.

"You keep disappearin' on me. Where do you go?"

"I never leave you. You just get distracted, that's all. But I'm always there..."

She didn't question his answer, wanting to make the most of the moment. But the moment would be brief. A few minutes passed and she heard what she thought were screeching birds overhead. She looked up as the sound became louder and louder and suddenly her vision went black. The sound of loud squeaky brakes climaxed until it lessened and stopped. She heard the sound of a car door and the click of a latch, and was instantly blinded by the morning sun.

"I don't see why this is necessary now, it seems risky."

Gil ignored his friend's warning, and reached down toward Lottie. "Have a heart, Nick, for cryin' out loud! She's probably suffered monoxide asphyxiation by now." After driving for several hours they had stopped off the two-lane highway at an old rest area with picnic tables and an outhouse. Gil pulled the duct tape off of Lottie's mouth as gently as he could.

"What if she starts screamin', man, what then?"

Gil looked back at Nick as if he were on the verge of strangling him.

Nick backed off, and decided to take a walk to the outhouse and stretch his aching back. When he came back he found Gil and Lottie sitting at one of the picnic tables across from each other. Lottie looked dazed and disoriented. Gil had attempted to start a conversation, but she had been unable to communicate beyond simple hand and head gestures. But the two of them made strong eye contact and didn't so much as look up at Nick or acknowledge his presence. That made him uneasy. "So, what's the deal, man?"

Gil resented the intrusion, but ignored his feelings and answered his partner in crime. "She's obviously quite weak right now. I was barely able to get her over here. I say we have her ride in the car with us."

Nick shook his head and rolled his eyes. "I think that's a bad idea, man. We agreed to keep her in the trunk, remember? We've-"

Gil interrupted, finally looking up at Nick. "Listen, you heartless bastard, I'm not about to treat someone like that. What we've done already is bad enough. You're gonna find yourself on your own, if you keep this shit up!"

Lottie suddenly interjected. "STOP! Please stop!"

Their mouths dropped as they looked at her.

Lottie breathed heavily as she continued in a weak raspy voice. "Who are you?!... What do you want?!... Wh-... why have you brought me here?!" As tired and frightened as she was, she felt angry. It had taken a good month's worth of indignities to get her to the point at which she felt that emotion. Fear had given way to anger, but both involved a plethora of tears.

Gil responded with his own tears. "I'm sorry. I'm so sorry..." He felt ashamed.

Nick was temporarily speechless.

Lottie struggled to her feet, took a few swaggering steps, and fell unconscious to the ground.

Nick hung his head and sat down at the picnic table. "Alright. She can ride in the car..."

· 9 ·

The late morning sun flooded through the window of Anna's living room in her efficiency-sized assisted living apartment, as she prayed silently on her prayer rope. This was despite the fact that the shade had been pulled. The mighty sunlight found edges, cracks and crevices through which to impose its presence, thereby giving the worn shade a hearty run for its money. The shade did, however, darken the room sufficiently to facilitate her prayer. She opened her eyes as the sound she had been waiting for occurred, a delicate double-rap on the apartment door.

"Come in, Sam."

Sam Crowfeather entered with a smile, charmed once again that his aged mother somehow knew that he was coming, despite his having informed no one of his intentions to visit. "Hi Ma!"

Anastasia struggled to her feet and embraced her son, delighted, as usual, by his presence. "Oh, goodness, what a blessing! What took you so long?"

"What? You were expecting me at a particular time?"

"Oh, I suppose not. You know me... always impatient."

"I know you as the person who taught me patience."

"Can I get you anything to drink?"

"Some cold water, if you have any."

Anna walked to her tiny kitchen. Since her husband's recent death, there were two things in her life that the ravages of grief and dementia hadn't affected, her Russian Orthodox faith, and her relationship with her son. She took great pleasure in Sam's attention to her in her declining years, and remained committed to his well-being and spiritual upliftment. She carried two glasses of water into the living room, handing one to her son.

As for Sam, he continued to seek counsel from his mother, and to enjoy her company. He smiled at her as she sat down and looked intently into his eyes from across the room, as was customary during his visits.

"You have something to tell me, don't you?"

"Well, Ma, as a matter of fact, I do. I was at Wounded Knee recently-"

"The Sundance?" she interjected with a smile.

"Yes."

"I suspected so. You have that glow that your father used to have... but I can sense that part of you may be troubled."

"Well, I don't want to spring my troubles on you, Ma. How have you been? How are they treating you here?"

"I'm fine, thank you. Even happier, now that you're here. As for springing your troubles, you know that's nonsense! I live for our discussions. Tell me what's troubling you."

Sam took a deep breath and thought about how to start. "Do you have any memories of Pa's vision quest experiences?"

"Well, of course he went through the actual experiences alone, but he was always peaceful when he returned, partly due to just being weak from deprivation of nourishment. But he always returned with a certain clarity of thought, and with a loving spirit toward me. I always looked forward to his return. It seemed as if it was those experiences that taught him to listen. We became closer with each passing year, because he learned to listen." Anna reached for a handkerchief on the table next to her chair, having become teary-eyed.

"I'm sorry, Ma."

"Don't be. I'm fine."

"Should I change the subject?"

"Don't you dare. You still haven't gotten around to the point."

"Okay, well... did he ever talk to you about his encounters with the Spirit?"

"Yes, but not in great detail. Those experiences are intensely personal."

Sam looked out the window. "Okay if I open the shade a little more?"

"Of course."

Sam opened the shade and sat back down, looking pensive. "Did Pa ever seem like a changed man after vision quest or Sundance experiences?"

"Only in the sense that he was more at peace with his life as a result. Why do you ask?"

"Well, Ma, on the one hand I feel closer to God than I ever have, but in another way I feel as if I'm going through a sort of..."

"What? A sort of what?"

"For want of better words, I guess you could call it an 'identity crisis'."

Anna looked lovingly at her son. "Sam, as you know, I'm not a Sioux Indian like your father, so I can't speak with great knowledge about Native American spirituality. I can tell you from my own experience, however, that God tends less to impart self-knowledge directly than he does to open up a process of discovery, to point his beloved creatures in a certain direction. I suspect that He would prefer to facilitate your journey, rather than to spoon-feed it to you. Despite the fact that none of us can succeed without

God's help, he wants us to take initiative, however feeble it may be."

"Hmmm. Perhaps the assignment is more momentous than I realized."

"Assignment?"

"What I mean is that, for some reason, I haven't been able to be at peace with my ancestry. I suppose there are people who have divergent lineages that don't think anything of it, but I feel tugged in two directions. I see the extraordinary outward world that the Europeans have created on this continent and feel drawn toward it. At the same time I feel drawn to an inner life that you and Pa impressed upon me at an early age... I feel unable to follow both urgings. They seem mutually exclusive."

"And you feel as if you have to make a choice?"

"Yes, I'd say that's it, although the idea of making a choice could just be a ruse of some sort, some means of keeping me off kilter."

Anna listened to her son thoughtfully. She'd watched him struggle with various forms of this seeming dilemma since his childhood, but somehow knew that he was destined to do so, perhaps because she had gone through something similar when faced years ago with the prospect of marrying a Native American. Her traditional Russian parents had strongly objected at the time, but her love for the proud Sioux man had prevailed. Memories of the young, handsome, Samuel the first, Sam's father, began to wash over her, before she looked back at her son quizzically. "What did you mean about the 'assignment'?"

"I don't know, Ma. This one's rather weird. I probably shouldn't have said anything."

"Now listen to you, becoming secretive around your dear old mother. Of all things!" Anna was, however, confident that she could get it out of him. Once Sam's heart was appealed to and awakened, it was her experience that he would always come clean.

She would just use a circuitous route, as she often had before. Soften him up, so to speak. "Do you remember when you were a boy, that brawl you walked away from at school?"

"You mean Johnny Dawkins?"

"Yes, I believe that was his name."

"What about it?"

"Your father was so disappointed at the time that you didn't let him have it."

"Yes, I remember."

"He later came around to seeing it my way. You were so courageous in that situation. You would have prevailed, but you just walked away."

"Well, I'm not certain I would have prevailed, but thank you for saying so. What does this have to do with the subject at hand?"

"Now you didn't let me finish!"

"I'm sorry, go ahead."

"Do you remember what happened after that?"

"My memory is vague."

"He went and complained, blaming you for instigating the situation. They sent you to the principal's office, and in the face of his bald-faced lie you took responsibility for the whole thing. You were suspended, despite the fact that you were blameless, remember?"

"Uhh, kind of..."

"You felt sorry for Johnny, and took the whole situation upon yourself."

"Well, as I remember, he was a pretty messed-up kid, on the verge of permanent suspension if he got in any more trouble. But I still don't understand what this has to do with anything."

"Let me finish. You demonstrated a charitable spirit then, and I suspect that remains with you to this day. You were an only child, Sam. With my faulty reproductive system, the doctors considered your birth a miracle. I don't think there are any coincidences in life, Sam. Having no brothers or sisters to share with, there was a danger of you becoming selfish and self-possessed. There's a psychobabble word I'm searching for..."

Narcissistic?"

"Yes, I believe that's it! You could have turned into a narcissist, and indeed, from time to time, I observed you being that way, but the better part of you eventually prevailed. And here you are now with an 'identity crisis.' Well, I suppose that all of us have a need for identity, but beyond a certain point, too much focus on one's identity can become self-indulgent. How do we 'find ourselves,' Sam? What is our purpose here?" She noticed him looking down at the floor again.

"Are you listening?"

"Yes Ma, go on."

"The danger is that the more one searches for identity, the further away one can get, because the focus is too much on self. In that moment years ago, you found your identity. We find ourselves through living a virtuous life, Sam. When we sacrifice our wants and desires and focus on the needs of others, we find our identity. To do anything else is to get sidetracked from the real purpose of life. So, what is this 'assignment?'"

Sam wondered how much he should reveal to her and looked down again at the floor. "I've been asked to find someone who has disappeared into the wild."

Anna let a moment pass while pondering her son's situation. "Well, the Spirit may well have put this responsibility on your plate. So go find him, but not at the expense of your soul. Who must you find, might I ask?"

Sam continued to look down at the floor.

"Sam, please look at me... who do you have to find?"

Sam looked up and his eyes were locked into his mother's gaze. If the past was any indication, she would see it in him, and he was reticent to divulge any more. Just as he was considering whether he should leave, his mother spoke.

"Oh my goodness, Elliot Teagartin?"

Sam didn't respond, but she could see it in his eyes that she had guessed correctly. He stood up and walked to his mother to embrace her. "I should leave, Ma, but I'm staying locally, if you want to get together again. And, keep in mind that the invitation for you to live with me in the city still stands, if you ever get tired of this place."

Anna held onto her son for a minute before letting go. "Be at peace, Sam, and do what you must. I have no doubt that you'll find him."

They stood at the doorway for an awkward moment before Sam turned to leave. Anna watched Sam walk down the path from her door, before the mother in her couldn't help but speak. "But Sam..."

"Yes, Ma?"

She looked at him imploringly. "Be careful."

· 10 ·

They were a thorn in his side, a festering wound, and a damnable nuisance, at that! Elliot had truly become rattled for the first time in... well, out here it was the first time. As a result, some of the creatures in his party were, albeit quietly, beginning to question the veracity of his avatar status. He had confirmed that it was the moose who'd been repeatedly stealing vital material goods from their village. His spies, the coyotes, had sufficiently established that fact. He'd sent emissaries, the gentle deer, in an attempt to cajole the moose with promises, pledges to grant them a special honorary status within the community, should they opt for membership. But alas, none of Elliot's appeals had been met with success.

The moose had become his Achilles' heel. In all of his years in the so-called "civilized world" of bricks and mortar, he had never contended with so formidable an opponent. He found himself taking to excessive drink in his exasperation, a tendency to which he had not, until now, surrendered. There was, however, one tool left in his toolbox, one remaining weapon in his arsenal. The coyotes had reported that the moose appeared to be struggling with comprehending the proper employment of the pilfered devices. It was in this failure on their part that he saw his opportunity. If he were to use their own strategy against them, to infiltrate the moose in an unsuspecting manner so as to unravel for them the mystery of utilization, he might be able to gradually pull them in his direction, toward submission, conformity, and assimilation. The moose needed to be convinced, once and for all, that salvation could happen only through him, that Elliot was the way, the means through which they could solve their existential dilemma. The moose would thereby have no alternative but to yield to his authority.

To accomplish this feat, an exceptional individual had to be found, one skilled in advanced extra-sensory communication, and in the art of subtle persuasion. Over the past few days he had spent less time in leisure, and more time inspecting the troops, observing his followers to find his ace in the hole. All he'd been able to establish up to this point was that the candidate would not be found amongst the mammals, for none could be found with the required subtlety of manner to ensure success. He would have to explore other possibilities.

"Hmmmm..." he thought. "Now who could it be?"

The moose hadn't given up, that is, with respect to the ghetto blaster. They'd waited a few days until the memory of the previous episode wasn't as intimidating. It had been kept in a special place in their surroundings, an area reserved for things for which they felt a certain reverence. It was a burial ground in which their predecessors had been laid to rest under branches, laden with berries and flowers, a delightful touch that had been observed vicariously at Elliot's encampment, and thereupon adopted into their funereal practice. When they felt the time was right, one of them was solemnly selected to retrieve the device and the rest of them gathered around.

With trepidation, the "Chosen One" brought the Ghetto Blaster forward, placed it in the pasture, and reached over and pressed the knob. This time white noise was heard at a medium volume, which was somewhat irritating, but not overly threatening. All of them stood by befuddled. A few minutes passed before they gradually began to hear what they thought was a faint voice. The sound was picked up by some other sensory faculty than their ears, and had a peculiar quality, a vibration. They looked around at each other as if to inquire who among them may have uttered the voice. "Not me..." all of them seemed to indicate.

The Chosen One leaned down closer to the ghetto blaster, but the voice could not be discerned amid the white noise, and seemed to be coming from another source. The utterance became clearer. "...Turn the dial... turn the dial..." This meant nothing to them at first, that is, with the exception of the Chosen One. He detected another knob on the side of the device, and through some mysterious intuition a mental connection was made between that knob and the voice.

"...Turn the dial..." he heard again. He reached down and touched it and nothing happened. Through a process of fiddling he finally noticed that it rotated in a circular fashion and the white noise ceased.

"...Turn the dial..." the voice implored again with more urgency. He turned the knob a little more and the sound of a biped could be heard, "Welcome to Performance Today!..." and the radio voice continued. The Chosen One reached down to turn the knob again, but a mysterious force restrained him.

And then it began, the sound of Handel's Messiah. The moose rejoiced with a collective cheer and began to delight in the music, all of them, that is, except the Chosen One. He was not willing to completely give himself over until he discovered the source of that extra-sensory voice, whose vibrations were still resounding in him. He perused the premises amid his brothers and sisters who were swaying and dancing, entranced as they were with Handel. There seemed to be nothing on the ground that would explain the mystery.

He then looked up and surveyed the trees around them and there it was, a large copperhead snake curled around a branch feasting on cicadas. Its head drooped down toward him and its serpentine eyes connected with his. The vibrations intensified and he found himself unable to look away or move until he heard the voice again. "At ease, at ease, my child... enjoy the music, seize the moment... I am Balar, there's more to come..."

Cale sat at the bar in the Delmonica Taproom trying to cool down after arguing heatedly with his boss. He could get in trouble for walking out of the office in the middle of the day, but he was beyond caring. Let George do what he will. Cale was a man obsessed. He'd first met his friend and mentor Artie during his college years when he'd taken a controversial class in "Gonzo Journalism," studying the antics of such fringe characters as Hunter S. Thompson, and others.

Arthur Dinsmore, the esteemed moderator of the course, considered himself as one in the tradition of such dubious luminaries, and had caused a stir when his writings contended that the lineage of this tradition could be traced back to Edward J. Murrow himself. Cale remembered his friend as one who felt as if freelancing was the only credible alternative to getting co-opted, swallowed up by the seductions of corporate culture... and then spit out as a puppet, a whipping boy with paper and pen, spewing out their spin like a good little robot, thereby serving the interests of billionaires.

Artie was on an endless quest for "truth," and would take any risk, uncover any snake under a rock in the interests of enlightening the public, shaking them out of their doldrums and complacency. When Artie came to work at the Tribune, as a favor to the owner of the Times who was a friend of George Cromwell's, it was like a dream come true to Cale. No one had impressed him more than Arthur Dinsmore during his years at the university, and now he had a chance to learn at the master's feet. The two of them had quickly become inseparable, which irritated George Cromwell to no end. Deep down, however, George had to have known that he had on his staff roster not only one of the best field reporters of the contemporary era, Artie Dinsmore, but a diamond in the rough, Calen Foster. Cale had to admit to himself that he wouldn't want to be in George's shoes, responsible for the behavior of these two neer-do-wells. And he also understood that George was worried about him becoming another freelancer through Artie's influence, thereby making the boss's job doubly stressful. But Calen was very much his own man, and he was angry with George for his intransigence regarding Artie's disappearance. His boss seemed spineless to him right now, and as such, he was disappointed in this man that he had once respected.

Cale remembered a part of a conversation he'd had early on with his mentor, word for word, as if it was yesterday, as if Artie's pronouncement was burned forever into his grey matter:

"...We've built an entire machine around the public's proclivity for 'celebrity worship,' a tendency for which we are largely responsible. It's a huge part of what drives everything in our world. 'Journalism,' a once respectable vocational institution, is slowly degenerating into a show-bizzy, glitzy, glamorous conundrum, an escapism that's unbecoming of our profession. We should be ferreting out the truth of the major life and death issues of our day, rather than rubbing the public's nose in sleaze. The corporate powers that be, who own most, if not all, of the news organizations in the country are intent on pulling the public ever more down a slippery slope toward the lowest common denominator, rather than striving to elevate the public toward a noble pursuit of truth..."

"Okay, I understand and agree... but where does this leave us? What should we be doing about it?"

"Look, Calen, this work is all I know, and I'm not going

to single-handedly change the fact that people live vicariously through celebrities. The people of this time are like children on a playground, being called in from recess by teachers with bags of candy in their hands. The public follows the suggestion of the mass media with regard to these movie actors, rock stars, mega-athletes, and people like Teagartin. Essentially they're doing one of two things, either putting these individuals up on pedestals and worshiping them like Gods, or knocking them off with as much tenacity and passion as when they put them up. The worst kind of escapism is the worship. The scandal involved in knocking them down isn't much better, but at least that way they see these people as human beings, with flaws like the rest of us. The celebrities are unfortunate victims of this 'media wheel' and all of its machinations. But to see them as 'real people' is far healthier for the public, in my humble opinion. So, I'll tell you where this leaves me. I'm going to serve the general public by focusing on the underbelly of celebrity culture. There's at least some truth to be found in that..."

Cale was stuck on one phrase of Artie's in this conversation – "...people like Teagartin..." People like Teagartin. He had been reading through articles written by Artie over the years at the Times and the Tribune. The material was all over the map. Profiles of corporations and the disastrous effects of their industrial behaviors upon the environment, as well as stories about the countless citizens throughout the world who'd been legally and financially plundered by their amoral interests, and who'd had their health ruined, and their lives forfeited, in the interests of "progress," as the corporations themselves define it; a four-part expose on the Metropolitan Police Department, which uncovered corruption to the core, and caused heads to roll; and numerous other articles on this country's institutions, not a slouch in the bunch.

And then there were the stories on celebrities – movie stars, rock gods, athletes, politicians, economists and corporate moguls. Yes... economists and corporate moguls – if there was one celebrity that Artie seemed to gravitate back to time after time, it was Elliot Teagartin. Artie had once commented that there was no one individual in contemporary America around whom more mystique revolved, who was more representative of what most white-collar men aspired to be, and yet at the same time was elusive and mysterious, which only reinforced the mystique, and made him seem all the more "cool" to men and women alike. It seemed to Cale as if Artie was determined to bring Teagartin down, and in doing so, to expose his brand of the "American Dream" as the charade that it was.

Artie had spoken to Cale on the phone about a potentially huge story he'd uncovered on his own. He hadn't revealed anything to anyone, but made plans to meet Cale for dinner in a week, indicating that the story was too big for him alone, and he needed help with it. He wanted to bring Cale in on the story, but then disappeared. The police had found his car at LaGuardia Airport, but no record could be found that he'd taken any commercial flights out of the city at that time. His name wasn't on any of the flight rosters. In relation to all of this, there was one thing in particular that ate away at Cale's thoughts. He couldn't quit thinking about it, and getting to the bottom of Artie's disappearance had taken on the importance of an almighty cause as a result. The time that Artie turned up missing? It was the same time that Teagartin's plane went down in the Northern Wilderness.

· 11 ·

Sam Crowfeather was enjoying a rare break from work. He'd recently had more transport jobs than he could handle, but the schedule had eased over the past few days, granting him some extra time to do some minor repairs on the plane. He was now preparing to make a pass over the Northern forests to find the wreckage of Elliot's plane. Landing in that area would be difficult, but necessary if he expected to track the whereabouts of the survivor. Such clues may enable him to narrow down the search somewhat, for the total area in which the survivor could conceivably be found was vast. Without some preliminary detective work he could spend weeks, even months, searching for him. From reading the material in the dossier he knew only approximately where the plane went down, so finding the crash site could take some time as well.

He jumped into the cockpit, turned on the engine, and proceeded down the runway. It was a beautiful day, with deep blue skies and little in the way of clouds or other moisture to obscure his view. He felt that familiar but awesome rush come over him as he became airborne. Sam was never more at peace with himself and at one with the earth and its elements than when he was flying. When the plane reached a proper altitude, he flew northward for a few hours and then engaged the autopilot for a brief moment to go back and fetch his binoculars. When he returned to the cockpit there was some mild turbulence, and as he sat back down he felt an odd sensation, as if he was not alone. He nearly jumped out of his seat upon hearing a voice.

"Don't be afraid."

Sam turned and there sat the Witness. Before he had a chance to ask who or how, the bearded figure pointed out the window.

"There... down there..."

Sam tore his stunned gaze away and looked out the window to his left, seeing what appeared to be the strewn-about wreckage of a plane. He grabbed the binoculars for a closer look. "You're right, that looks like the site... how did you-" Sam turned again to his right and his uninvited guest had vanished. He put on the autopilot again and quickly searched the plane. The Witness was nowhere to be seen, but Sam continued to feel a presence other than his own. He had no time to ponder this occurrence further, however, for he didn't want to lose the location of the crash site.

Sam circled the site, noting the coordinates on the control panel, and circled again in a wider arc. About two miles to the west was a large swath of grassland between the hills that appeared to be relatively flat and long enough for a landing. He would have to hike to the crash site. The landing was difficult to maneuver, but he sensed the lingering presence of the Witness, a steadying influence on his hands as he manned the controls and gradually brought the plane to a halt. He sat for a period of time before disembarking, contemplating what had happened. He was not prone to question his sanity in the midst of such an experience, being a strong believer in, and seeker of, the unseen dimensions of existence. His encounter with the Witness only reinforced his suspicion that there was something profound at work... something that Sam Crowfeather had been called upon by the unseen world to discover.

It took Sam a few hours to forge through the hilly hardwood forest to the first piece of wreckage he found, a small piece of the wing. It wasn't long before he found more pieces of the plane. Of course, everything germane to the crash investigation had been removed from the site, along with the remains of the deceased passenger. From what was left, however, he found himself doubting whether anyone could have survived. The plane appeared to have exploded into many small pieces, and there must have been a lot of fuel in the plane, judging from how charred the trees and foliage were in the area presumed to be the point of impact. Even if the person had survived, it seemed inconceivable that he could have been in enough of one piece to live for long, let alone to embark upon a trek through the forest.

Sam stopped and reminded himself that these suspicions were beside the point, because someone must have survived if the dossier information was correct, and he needed to find clues as to the direction this individual might have gone. He spent a few more hours perusing the site, but could not find anything resembling tracks or any other directional clues. The sun was beginning to dip down on the horizon, and he decided to get back to his plane while there was still some light. He took a more circuitous route back to the plane, still baffled by the lack of clues at the site.

While hiking through a valley he noticed something peculiar. It appeared that a grave of some sort had been dug in a clearing in the forest up ahead. Foul play was the only explanation he could muster to explain an unmarked grave in such a remote region. He reached the clearing and retrieved a machete from his backpack. He probed into the disturbed earth and rooted around. The machete caught onto something. He attempted to pry whatever it was out of the ground. A piece of thick white fabric was forcibly exposed. He continued to unearth the fabric until he knew what he'd found – a parachute.

By the time he was finished he'd retrieved evidence of several parachutes, and found his explanation for the lack of clues at the crash site, not to mention the answer to how the other passenger had survived. Someone must have parachuted out of the plane before the crash, along with a considerable stash of equipment. He walked around the vicinity of the "gravesite," and before long he found what he was looking for – evidence of tracks leading in a northwesterly direction. He marveled at how he had stumbled upon this grave, and then that feeling welled up in him again. It had evolved into a peaceful sensation, a quiet gentle reassurance. He was not alone.

What Sam learned early on in his association with the Witness was that his presence could be felt just as strongly when Sam couldn't see him, and that the division between inner dialog and spoken conversation could blur at the drop of a hat. It took him a little time to get accustomed to this, however. As he hiked back to the plane, Sam thought about the newspaper accounts he'd read about Elliot's supposed "village in the wild." He tried to imagine the degree of planning and organization it would take to parachute out of a plane with all the materials needed to transform a wilderness in accordance with his own standards of suitability.

And then Sam's thought received a palpable reply, "You know, he may have made more than one trip out here..." and he became suddenly aware that he was walking side-by-side with the Witness, who continued, "The skill of such an individual is often in how he leaves the impression of something miraculous. It appeals to our general fascination with 'smoke and mirrors.' At times, our infatuation with trickery can reach the point to which we are missing the obvious." The two stopped and faced each other as the Witness extended his hand. "I've waited long for this moment, Sam."

As he felt a subtle surge of energy from the handshake, Sam, clearly tongue-tied, searched for a response.

The Witness smiled. "Relax, Sam... at ease, I won't bite."

"Forgive me... so you think he may have dropped some of the stuff on a previous occasion?"

They continued forward through the brush. The Witness knew that one of his first tasks with the new protégé would be to demystify the situation as much as possible, considering the media circus that prevailed. "Well, it's certainly a strong possibility that other excursions were undertaken, don't you think? For one thing, the plane was only so big and could hold only so much material."

"Well, I guess you may have a point there... so, can I lay to rest, then, that this is Elliot Teagartin we're talking about here? Who was the other passenger?"

"My advice, Sam, would be to avoid concern over who the other passenger is or was. There are others contending with that issue as we speak. You're headed in the right direction now, don't get side-tracked. Oh, and by the way, your mother sends her regards, and I'd like to add my voice to her parting sentiment, by all means, be careful!" And in the wake of that solemn message, the Witness passed into the invisible realm.

· 12 ·

Cale was on his way back to the office, bracing himself for another meeting with George Cromwell. Despite the fact that he now had what he felt to be solid evidence linking Artie's disappearance to Elliot Teagartin's ill-fated plane flight to the Northern Wilderness, he felt unsure about Cromwell's reaction. Should he reveal this evidence to George, or shouldn't he? He had already requested to do a piece on Teagartin on two previous occasions, but George had refused to allow it, feeling that Cale's motives centered too much around Artie's disappearance, and not enough around the intent to produce solid investigative journalism. George did not like reporters letting stories become too personal to them, expecting instead a spirit of relative detachment. Cale seemed to him to be in way over his head on this one, to the point of the endeavor becoming a vendetta.

What Cale didn't know, however, was that George had received a phone call yesterday from corporate headquarters. They expressed strong concern over the Tribune's silence regarding the ongoing media coverage on Elliot Teagartin. His superiors felt that the Tribune was risking the loss of reader share, thereby losing ground to competitors, most notably to the Times, the other news organization in the city. Though they hadn't directly ordered him to do anything, there was a palpable undertone to the conversation that made it clear to George that he'd better jump into the fray. This exasperated him considerably, for two reasons. Firstly, he detested the kind of sensational journalism that had surrounded the coverage on Teagartin, and felt that the Tribune should, as a matter of principle, maintain the high ground and keep silent. Secondly, the only reporter who could handle the story with the kind of finesse necessary to avoid such tabloid nonsense was Calen Foster.

Blessed with some extra time before the meeting with George, Cale stopped at a diner to get some coffee and review the evidence. He had just come from the residence of Artie's sister, Nicole, with whom Artie had been very close. Nicole was heartbroken over her brother's disappearance, and angry in response to the lackluster investigation by the Police, who, she was convinced, had unofficially dropped the matter. She suspected that ill will lingered among the Police toward Artie as a result of his exposé on the Department that had exposed corruption and caused a massive shake-up in the ranks.

It was Nicole who had steered Cale toward a friend of hers who was a disgruntled employee of LaGuardia Airport, where the Police had found Artie's car. From the beginning, Cale could not figure out why Elliot Teagartin's car was found at LaGuardia, when he notoriously always flew out of JFK. This friend of Nicole's, for a fee and under the condition of anonymity had informed Cale that Teagartin owned a private hangar at LaGuardia, where he came and went undetected. He thereby used LaGuardia as his means of escape when he wished to avoid public exposure of his whereabouts. Elliot's influence and power enabled him to shroud his travel from LaGuardia.

Another bit of evidence Nicole had exposed to Cale was a cassette tape that Artie had given her for safekeeping. On the cassette was a recently recorded interview with none other than

Elliot Teagartin:

> <u>A.D.</u> "This is an interview with Mr. Francis Elliot Teagartin, March 30, 1981, 7pm. So, 'Elliot', if I may refer to you by your first name... are we on a first name basis?"
>
> <u>E.T.</u> "I would certainly hope so by now..."
>
> <u>A.D.</u> "So... how many times have I interviewed you over the years? 10? 15?"
>
> <u>E.T.</u> "Oh, goodness... I've lost count..."
>
> <u>A.D.</u> "Tell me... what's new in the life of Elliot Teagartin?"
>
> <u>E.T.</u> "Oh... my kingdom for that which is new!"
>
> <u>A.D.</u> "...Now, from where I sit, that's a rather puzzling statement! A man like yourself, with your fabulous wealth... it would seem that anything's possible!"
>
> <u>E.T.</u> "What, exactly, are you inferring?"
>
> <u>A.D.</u> "Well... you could travel to the ends of the earth... offer your counsel to leaders anywhere around the globe... play a part in the economic invigoration of Third World countries... whether it's business or pleasure, I could imagine an endless potential for new vistas... new experiences..."
>
> <u>E.T.</u> "Oh please... spare me the drivel, (the sound of a yawn) ...you're putting me to sleep!"
>
> <u>A.D.</u> "...Are you honestly telling me that there's nothing of interest to you in anything I just said?"
>
> <u>E.T.</u> "Honestly, I've been hinting to you that I am profoundly bored..."
>
> <u>A.D.</u> "Now...that's just inconceivable to me. There are countless people who would give anything to be in your shoes."

E.T. "Well, that's just the thing... their assumptions are erroneous, to say the least... they just don't know..."

A.D. "Explain yourself... explain what you mean..."

E.T. "You know that saying... I don't recall who exactly said it... that most men lead lives of quiet desperation?"

A.D. "Yes?"

E.T. "Well, if the truth be known, most men have no concept of 'quiet desperation' until they've stood in the shoes of someone like yours truly..."

A.D. "Okay... go on..."

E.T. "...They simply have no idea. When one possesses great wealth and invests it in the activities you mentioned previously... traveling... giving counsel... uplifting, etc, etc... one finds that the world is indeed a rather small place, and the possibilities for new experiences are finite..."

A.D. "...So translate this into simple human terms for me..."

E.T. "...Well, as I said... I'm bored to my bones... it feels as if there's little of consequence left for me. I've engaged myself to a point of depletion... the cup that previously 'runneth over' hath 'run dry', so to speak. And now, as you see, I'm sitting here being interviewed far past my prime, devising a clever means of repeating myself..."

A.D. "...But, surely there's something notable going on in your life. How about your new book? Tell me about that..."

E.T. "Well... it's an account..."

A.D. "Yes... go on..."

E.T. "It contains various profiles of men I've

known over the years, world leaders, economists, philosophers, and the like..."

A.D. "Does it include any underworld figures?"

(a pause...)

E.T. "...Excuse me?"

A.D. "I get the distinct impression that you heard me. Should I repeat myself?"

(an awkward, tense silence...)

E.T. "Just what the hell are you suggesting?"

A.D. "Well... specifically, I'm referring to Mr. Escobar. Tell me about him..."

(another awkward silence...)

E.T. "...I think you should turn the tape recorder off..."

A.D. "...And why would you want me to do that?"

E.T. "...For the simple reason that it feels to me as if you are engaging in a game of entrapment..."

A.D. "Look... I have no idea why you may have had contacts with Mr. Escobar, what your motives were, what you may have been trying to accomplish... that's what I'm attempting to uncover..."

E.T. "I don't think you're being entirely honest with me. Where, pray tell, did you get this information?"

A.D. "You know I can't divulge my sources..."

E.T. "Then why, might I ask, would you expect me to be forthright?"

A.D. "Perhaps we should change the subject. But before we do so, would it be possible to take up this matter in a future interview?"

(another tense, awkward silence...)

E.T. "I might be willing to grant another interview, providing that I would choose the time and the place."

(shuffling noises as if the interview is coming to a close...)

<u>A.D.</u> "Agreed. You'll get in touch with me then?"

<u>E.T.</u> "You'll hear from me, Arthur... Good night, then..."

<u>A.D.</u> "Good night."

(tape recorder clicks off...)

Cale was convinced that Teagartin may have lured Artie into a leisurely plane flight where the interview he'd promised would occur, intending only to do him in. Artie, it seemed, may have come too close to the real Elliot Teagartin, and paid dearly for it. Cale knew that he lacked details about Elliot's association with this "Escobar," but felt he had enough to spur a further investigation, if only George would relent. One last point which lent credence to Cale's suspicions – the news coverage on Teagartin thus far had repeatedly speculated about the corpse found in the wreckage of Elliot's plane being that of a member of a crime syndicate. Cale was convinced that this theory didn't hold water, for the simple reason that if Elliot had brazenly murdered a criminal of this sort, why was there no evidence that the criminal organization had come after Elliot in retaliation? It wasn't like them to ignore someone having "offed" one of their own, even if the murderer was someone as powerful as Elliot Teagartin. There had also been nothing whatsoever in the news about a missing crime lord. Who was it, then, if the tabloid accounts had been correct? Cale finished his coffee and arrived a few minutes late for his meeting with Cromwell. He entered George's office, and immediately went right to the point. "George, I insist on doing an on-going piece on Elliot Teagartin, and before you say no, I've-"

"Cale, close the door." Cale complied with Cromwell's request and turned around to face George, who began to speak without giving Cale a chance to continue. "Go ahead and do the piece."

Cale was shocked.

"Don't forget, however, that I'm having you do a piece of objective journalism. I don't want any tabloid bullshit, and this is NOT, I repeat, this is NOT your opportunity to get even. Is there any part of this that you don't understand?"

"No, George, I understand." Cale left, closing the door gently this time. He was still amazed at how easily this had gone off. I guess the third time was the charm... he thought to himself. The third time was the charm...

· 13 ·

The three of them continued north, Nick and Gil in the front alternating with the driving duties, and Lottie in the back, mostly asleep. Late into the evening on their second day on the road, they stopped at a little greasy spoon for a bite to eat. Nick still felt nervous about the new traveling arrangement, but his fears were progressively allayed on the occasions when Lottie would awaken, sit up, and look out the window. She showed no signs whatsoever that she would bolt at the first opportunity. Lottie seemed like a lost soul who would just as soon be here with them as anywhere else. In fact, based upon their scant conversations thus far, she seemed vaguely relieved to have escaped her previous situation in the city.

On a previous occasion while Lottie was asleep, they had stopped at a convenience store for gas, and bought a newspaper, finding an article with the headline, "LOTTERY WINNER MISSING - FOUL PLAY SUSPECTED." A photograph of Lottie accompanied the article. Nick was perturbed at Gil for leaving the paper in the car where Lottie could find it. She looked at the article and it barely seemed to register. It was as if it was about someone else. What relieved Nick and Gil all the more was a lack of reference in the article to any particular suspects.

They assumed that this might mean that the kidnapping had been pulled off without a hitch, without any witnesses.

This article was further back in "Section A" of the paper, thereby playing second or third fiddle, along with other events of the day, to the headline "TEAGARTIN ENCLAVE SIGHTED IN NORTHERN WOODLAND." The two musicians had been following this ongoing saga with great interest, especially Gil, who'd seen Elliot speak at a forum during his college days. Being more "bohemian" in orientation, both Gil and Nick were a bit contemptuous toward Elliot's cultural philosophy and theories of economics. They were, nonetheless, intrigued by someone who would suddenly disappear into the bush as he did, assuming that the ongoing stories amounted to more than mere sensationalism.

A peculiar angle in this most recent write-up suddenly hit home to Gil. Recent stories seemed to loosely ride on the assumption that the charred corpse found in the wreckage of Elliot's plane was an underworld figure whom Elliot may have wanted dead, lending a tone of sinister desperation to the flight of Elliot Teagartin into the wilderness. It was this desperation that frightened Gil the most. He'd seen the same spirit of recklessness in his partner. He contemplated the thin line between genius and despair that appeared in such individuals as Nicolai and Elliot. Nick was on his own criminal flight into the wilderness, and what increasingly disturbed Gil was that he himself was an accomplice.

Strung out from the road, the three of them sat quietly at the diner eating their sandwiches. There arose what Nick considered a "down side" to Lottie's lack of concern over the kidnapping. She and Gil were obviously quite taken with each other. They looked at each other as if Nick was invisible. The implications of this development felt ominous to Nick, but he was powerless to do anything about it. When it came to women, Gil was a kid in a candy store, and there was no way to pull him away from an attraction. In the past, he'd simply let Gil's romances flame out, but Gil's infatuation with Lottie in the context of this situation only complicated the matter. He short-circuited the goo goo eyes by striking up a conversation as they were finishing their meal.

"So... what's the deal with your Dad?"

Lottie turned to Nick appearing rather confused. "What do you mean?"

"Well, if you'll pardon my saying it, he looked kinda looped back at the party."

Lottie turned away, her expression becoming sullen. "Yeah... well he's been gittin' worse since this lottery thing happened."

"Worse?"

"Well, he's always been a drunk, but now with all that money he hardly ever comes up fer air. I'm powerful worried 'bout him, but there ain't nothin' I can do. I heard tell from kin that he's been this way ever since Mama died, back when I was born. To be honest with you, I'm glad to get away from him for a spell..."

Gil chimed in. "Even under these circumstances?"

"Listen, y'all can have whatever you want. If I had some o' that money right now, I'd give it to you, all of it."

Nick was rather shocked at such generosity, but didn't necessarily doubt her sincerity. "Well, where's the money now?"

"I guess Daddy's got all of it. I 'magine he's back home by now, holed up with the pit bull, his shot gun, and his whiskey. If it were me, I wouldn't be messin' with him right now, but I'll give you the phone number if you want."

Nick pondered the predicament of having to extract ransom from such a character. He looked over at Gil. "We'd better go before someone recognizes her."

Gil and Lottie went back to the car while Nick settled up. They drove a few more hours until they were in need of sleep. Seeing an old mom and pop motel up the road, they stopped for the night. Lottie was the first to settle into the room and promptly fell asleep on one of the twin beds. Nick and Gil stood at the back of the car while Gil retrieved the foam mattress from the trunk for the one who would have to sleep on the floor.

Nick had been holding his tongue, but finally yielded. "Look, I can see what's happening between the two of you, and I don't suppose there's a lot I can do about it. All I ask is that you at least try and keep one of your eyes on the ball, okay? You don't seriously think you're gonna shack up with someone you've just kidnapped, do you?"

Gil looked back at Nick. He was too exhausted to respond. He'd taken his eyes off the ball from the moment he'd sat down yesterday at that picnic table with Lottie. He felt nothing but regret over what he and Nick had done. He no longer cared about the money, but as he looked into Nick's eyes, sensing once again the intense jumble of greed and longing, he just didn't have the heart to tell him.

They finally reached their planned destination after nearly three days of driving: a rustic cabin in the Northern woods owned by one of Nick's relatives. The two musicians had stayed there several times over the years as a means of getting away from the city and chilling out. The cabin had electricity and running water, but no phone service, lending them the quiet and privacy they needed to focus on their creative endeavors. They'd written music together in that cabin retreat, thereby cementing their relationship as music partners.

There had also been some ugly fights there, and alcohol usually played a part in these conflicts. The combination of Nick and excessive booze was volatile, and Gil had insisted that Nick swear an oath not to drink on this trip, to which Nick, somewhat tentatively, had agreed. Nicolai had broken such promises before, however, and although Gil was surprised at how calm his partner had seemed over the past few days, he was concerned that Nick awoke feeling depressed that morning at the motel, and had been rather moody throughout the last leg of their journey. He'd spent half the previous night out walking the roads in the vicinity of the motel, unable to sleep. Nick knew that Gil and Lottie had slept together, given the close quarters in the motel room, and he felt left out. He'd always felt like the odd man out during Gil's romantic flings, and couldn't wait for them to end. What little there was of his own love life had been a pitiful mess. Women were afraid of his intensity, and generally kept him at arm's length. As a child, Nick had suffered some abuse at the hands of his mother. His one great love affair during college had ended in despair, with him spending time in jail on battery charges, which were subsequently dropped by his ex-flame. He'd come out of these two formative experiences with somewhat of a misogynist orientation. He did his best to keep such emotions under wraps, due to the wretched memory of his college days in lock-up. However, Gil was well aware of this propensity, being essentially the only person on the planet that Nick confided in, and truly considered a friend.

Nick was not feeling too friendly toward Gil, however, when they'd arrived at the cabin. He suspected that Gil was losing heart with regard to carrying out the kidnapping scheme, and sensed that he may have to handle the ransom arrangements alone. Having relied on Gil over the years to keep him on a relatively even keel, he now felt out on a limb by himself, but he hadn't yet given up trying to salvage his friend's support. The nearest town was some fifteen miles down winding roads, and after they'd spent the night and the following morning in the cabin, Nick felt the time was drawing near for him to go into town to get supplies and make a ransom call. He sat on the front porch with Gil while Lottie was taking a bath.

"Listen, Gil, we don't have much food here, so I thought

I'd go into town. I suppose it would be best if you stayed here and kept an eye on Lottie. I wanna make a ransom call while I'm there... how much do you think we should demand?"

Gil was unable to respond. He resented being reminded of the reason that they'd gone there. He could only lean his head down into his hands. Nick felt the knot in his stomach growing tighter.

"C'mon, man, don't bail out on me now. I need you! We're in this together, remember?!" Gil looked up at his friend, feeling a mixture of anger and pity.

"Nick, you're asking me to steal from someone I've grown quite fond of. Do you realize that?"

"Well, yeah, that was the original idea, if you recall. Hell, Gil, she as much as offered us the money! You stand to gain in this thing as much as I do. We're doin' this for both of us, man, for both of us!"

"Nick, I can't do this... I'm in love with her!"

"Aww, c'mon, man, her and how many others over the years? You were in love with all of 'em, weren't you?! So what else is new? Gil... man, I need you! Gil?"

Gillian didn't know what to say, so he said nothing.

After a tense period of silence, Nick stood up and walked into the cabin. He retrieved the car keys from the coffee table, went back out and got in the car and left.

Gil watched him disappear down the dusty gravel road. Through his reticence, he feared that he may have just dealt a death knell to a fifteen year relationship with his best friend. He dreaded what may happen over the next 24 hours, but he'd been true to his heart. He'd made his choice.

· 14 ·

Daddy Crump swerved around a corner and skidded into the driveway in his brand-spankin'-new Ford Pickup with all the options. He'd just been at the dealership where he paid cash. He'd made a few reckless detours to the liquor store and Walmart on the way home, buying more booze and some kitchen appliances that he figured Lottie would want, that is, when she surfaced. He vaguely assumed she'd be back one of these days, and wanted her to have everything he presumed her little heart would desire. Daddy'd been confused over the disappearance of his daughter, finding it inconceivable that she'd want to walk away from the high-life, but also having difficulty swallowing the notion of foul play. He'd been so consistently inebriated over the past month and a half, that he didn't know how or what to think. His capacity for organized thought was rapidly disintegrating.

It took a few swaggering trips to get the appliances into the mobile home before he resumed his liquor-fest. On display in the middle of the living room sat another one of his recent purchases, a state-of-the-art mechanical bull. As always, the booze made Daddy stupid and silly, and he felt another notion spring up out of his pickled brain. The pit bull, who'd been reclining on the new sofa bed, could sense that something bad was about to happen, and ran down the hallway to hide in one of the bedrooms.

Daddy began to laugh uncontrollably as he set the appliances on the kitchen counter and at other locations throughout the living room. The cough-sputtered guffaws continued as he plugged the machines in, and turned 'em all on – the blender, food processor, juicer and the coffee grinder, along with the new automatic dishwasher that he'd just had installed. He continued cackling away while he staggered over to a metal trash can full of cash hidden behind the new La-Z-Boy. Retrieving the can, he set it on an end table next to the bull. The appliances continued to thrash away noisily as he grabbed his half empty fifth of Jack Daniels and mounted the bull, nearly falling off the other side. He started up the bull, chugged on the whiskey with one hand and grabbed wads of cash with the other, repeatedly throwing them into the air.

"Yeeeeeeeeeeeeee Haaaaaaaaaaaaw!!!!"

His shrill voice could be heard above the cacophony of appliances, all of which drowned out another sound that attempted to penetrate the decadent Bacchanalian spectacle – the telephone. At about the fifth ring, Daddy was suddenly gripped in pain, and clutched his abdomen. Dropping the open bottle, he fell off the bull onto the end table, knocking the can of cash onto the floor. He rolled off the end table onto the cash-laden, whiskey-soaked throw rug, having suffered a massive heart attack. As he lay dying in the cash and whiskey, the appliances continued their relentless chorus of white noise. The phone rang another five times and then stopped.

Nick slammed the phone down and repeatedly kicked the side of the phone booth. "No answer, no voicemail or message machine?!?" The tension had been building and his heart was racing. He needed some kind of quick relief or he was going to blow. It had been hard enough to feel abandoned by his friend, but having the ransom attempt go nowhere was more than he could take. Leaving the phone booth, he got in the car and headed for the tavern on the edge of town. He'd hang out for a while, cool down, and attempt the ransom call again, he told himself, frantically trying to avoid the nervous breakdown that he'd kept one step ahead of for years. Everything would be fine, he told himself. Everything would be fine. He'd try the call again later.

Lottie finished toweling herself, ran a comb through her hair and put her clothes back on. She walked through the cabin, out the front door and sat down on the porch swing next to Gil, noticing that the car was gone. Gil's appearance reminded her of a song that had been running through her head – "Man of Constant Sorrow." She looked lovingly at him. "Never saw a man cry before..."

Gil wiped his face with his hands and looked back at her. "Nick's gone into town to make a ransom call".

She put her head on his shoulder. "Now, don't you start that again, you done 'pologized enough already."

They stood up together and embraced. A few minutes passed, and she gently let go of his back and reached her hands up and wiped tears from under his eyes with her thumbs, feeling for the first time in her life what it was to comfort someone. She experienced what it was to be strong for someone else and to not be afraid. This was new ground for her – to care for someone like this, to be in love.

Strangely enough, this was new for Gil also. He'd loved a lot of women over the years, but no one quite like her, so lacking in pretense that she seemed to exude a natural beauty from within. She didn't seem to have an agenda or a plan as far as he could see. She spoke as if she was completely open-minded about the future, and utterly unspoiled by the millions she'd won. And now, she'd succeeded in pulling him out of his saddened state and restoring his equilibrium. He looked into her eyes, let go and stepped back, reaching his hand toward her. "You wanna go for a walk?"

She smiled and took his hand. They walked off into the forest, entering together into one of those rare moments in which everything felt right and all was at peace. They were happy. It was the calm before the storm.

Following a long romantic stroll through the woods, Gil and Lottie stepped back into the clearing next to the cabin, noticing that the car had returned. They walked up the driveway onto the porch and cautiously entered the cabin. Furniture was overturned and broken glass was on the floor. Gil thought about turning around that instant with Lottie and leaving, but years of habit made him stay the course. He felt as if he owed it to his friend to help restore him to a degree of calm, as he had on so many occasions over the past 15 years. He'd even half-hoped to talk Nick out of the kidnapping scheme altogether, considering that they didn't appear to have been implicated in the "foul play." They could go back home and proceed as if the whole crazy episode had never occurred. His eyes locked with Nick's as he found him sitting on the couch with a glass of rum and coke in his hand. On the coffee table in front of him was a fifth of Bacardi, nearly empty. The look on Nick's face was hostile, his eyes blood-shot and his lips quivering. To his horror, Gil saw something next to the bottle that quashed his hopes. It was a Saturday night special. Until now, guns had never been an element in these recurring melodramas.

Nick poured the rest of the rum into his glass. "Whazzamatter, BRO?!?... You don't think we can engage in felonious behavior without a fire arm, now do you?! HUH?!?" The venom in Nick's voice was frightening, reminding Gil of previous conflicts that had occurred in this domicile, though it seemed that Nick had stepped it up several notches this time. An ugly struggle seemed imminent. Out of the corner of his eye, Gil noticed the car keys near him on the counter and casually put his hand on them, easing them slowly into his pocket.

Nick continued loudly. "SO... NO RESPONSE AGAIN? HUH?!?"

Gil finally answered his friend in as serene a manner as he could muster. "What do you want me to say, Nick?"

"Honestly, I don't give a rat's ass what you have to say, BRO, but I'll tell you what we're gonna do. We're gonna pack up, throw the little hillbilly bitch back in the trunk, and head directly non-stop to 'Hickville.' I don't know why we didn't think of this before. We'll just get the money directly from Daddy the boozer!"

Seeing Nick reach for the gun, Gil reacted impulsively. He grabbed an open 2 liter Classic Coke from the counter and threw it at Nick, spraying cola throughout the room, and then lunged across the room at Nick, grabbing his arm, initiating a violent struggle for the gun.

Nick fought his friend with a fury. "I'M GONNA KILL YOU, YOU SNAIL-SUCKING SON OF A BITCH!!!"

As they feverishly writhed around on the couch, Gil called out to Lottie who helplessly stood by in shock. "RUN, LOTTIE!!! RUN!! GET OUT OF HERE!!!"

Lottie hesitated, fearing for Gil's life, but he continued to implore her with all the breath he had.

"GO!!!..."

She ran out the door and across the clearing into the woods.

Nick's rage continued. "COME BACK HERE, YOU YOKEL WHORE!!!..."

Lottie had run about 30 meters into the forest when she heard a gunshot. She started crying, but didn't stop, telling herself that there was little she could do but get in the way, and possibly get herself killed. She also didn't savor spending a long miserable broken hearted car ride in a cold dark trunk, assuming,

God forbid, that Nick had prevailed. Her fear had returned with a vengeance, and the fight-or-flight mechanism kept her on the move. She no longer looked back. She just kept running and said a prayer in her head for Gil.

Back at the cabin, Nick cried out in pain. A bullet had ripped through his shoulder at an angle just above the clavicle.

Gil was revolted at what happened and threw up on the floor. He couldn't bring himself to pick up the firearm that lay on the floor next to Nick, who appeared to be losing blood rapidly. In a panic, he wrapped Nick's shoulder with a towel and ran out to the car and left. Barreling down the road to find a telephone, Gil thought about the numerous movies he had seen over the years that contained the typical "struggle for the gun." He used to complain loudly about boring movie clichés. He wasn't yawning now.

Finding the lone infamous phone booth in town 15 minutes later, he placed an anonymous 911 call about a crazed individual with a gunshot wound. Quickly imparting the address, he promptly hung up. He raced back to the cabin, astonished to find it empty. Both Nick and the gun were missing. Too full of adrenaline to ponder what had happened, he grabbed his clothes and whatever food and drink he could find, stuffed them into a backpack, and ran outside. It was probably other movies he had seen that gave him the presence of mind to wipe his fingerprints off the door handles and steering wheel of the car and to lock it, keeping the keys.

Gil ran off into the forest to find Lottie, hearing sirens in the distance approaching the cabin. He kept moving through the forest trying to get as far away as he could before dark. His partnership with Nick was over, and he no longer mourned the loss, after all that had just happened. As his state of shock and horror gradually wore off, however, he had to admit to himself that he would, ironically, always owe his former friend a debt of gratitude.

Had it not been for Nicolai Zagorski's ill-fated kidnapping caper, he might never have met the love of his life.

. 15 .

Sam Crowfeather was in the air heading northwest, trying to stay below the clouds in order to see what was below. The Witness stood invisibly at his shoulder. Sam had become more acquainted with the Witness recently in his dreams, whereupon he had introduced Sam to a few individuals, one blonde woman and another individual with a backpack. He was uncertain who these people were, but knew only that he was being urged on an unseen level to keep on the lookout for them. This struck him as a piece of the puzzle, another part of a mystery whose significance was unfolding slowly before his eyes. Sam was, if nothing else, a man of faith. He didn't question the authority of the Witness, but, through some kind of supernatural connection, he trusted in his wisdom and guidance. He was an intuitive creature, and believed in his heart that a time was coming in which the light would shine fully, and he would understand.

Ten minutes had passed since he had seen an odd phenomenon in the forest below, a botanical contour that didn't fit the usual pattern one would see from the air. After circling the area, he noted what appeared to be an abandoned encampment of some sort. Continuing northwest, he looked for sources of water, figuring that whoever was out there would gravitate toward such an essential benefit. Through his binoculars Sam spotted a meandering stream, and followed its general course until he saw what appeared to be another encampment in the distance. Detecting movement on the ground, he felt prompted to turn around, wishing to keep as low a profile as possible. He was confident that he had found something worth investigating. He flew back to the previous location, and looked for a place to land. Spotting some flatland a few miles away he landed the plane.

Disembarking, he locked the plane, and turned around to begin his journey on foot. Before he could take a few steps, he noticed someone in the distance on horseback coming his direction. At that moment he regretted not having brought a firearm for protection, and made a mental note to do so in the future. As the figure came close, he recognized him. "Well, I'll be... Cale Foster! What are you doing out here?"

"I saw the plane and thought it may be you. What's new, Sam?"

"You answer my question first."

"Well, I'm looking for someone, but getting nowhere fast. I've been riding around this general area all morning. It feels as if I'm just going in circles..."

"You're looking for someone?"

"Now, that's no fair... why don't you tell me what you're doin' out here?"

Sam was eager to get going on his hike, and was uneasy about divulging information to a newspaper reporter this early in the investigation. He continued to press the point with Cale. "You say you're looking for someone, who might that be?"

"Sam, don't get me wrong here, but this contest of questions is getting rather lopsided, don't you think?"

Sam thought some more and concluded that they must be looking for the same person. Who else would Cale be looking for out here? "Okay, lemme guess, you're looking for Elliot

Teagartin?"

Cale chose a presumptuous response. "What a coincidence, that we run into each other out here, and we're both hunting down the same guy!"

Sam and Cale went back several years, to not long after Cale went to work at the Tribune. It had been a reciprocal relationship in which they'd come to count on each other for information regarding various investigations. Desiring to extricate himself from the untimely interaction, Sam put forth a proposition. "You're likely to continue spinnin' your wheels out here, the way you're goin' about it. I'll make you a deal. I'm definitely on to something here, but I'm running out of time, and need to continue on my own. How about us getting together in the future and sharing information?"

After wasting his time all morning, Cale was game. "I'm afraid I don't have much to offer at this point. Would you still be willing to talk?"

"Under one condition: my name isn't brought into it. Strictly anonymous."

Cale was elated. He'd always been able to count on Sam in the past, and if he could get more specific information about the location of Teagartin, he'd be eternally grateful. "Deal! I'll call you some time over the next week."

Sam was relieved. "Sounds like a plan."

Cale turned the horse around and galloped away. Sam watched him disappear into the distance before setting off on a trek to the abandoned encampment to look for clues.

From there he would follow the trail to what he hoped to be Elliot Teagartin's current enclave.

The hike was relatively easy at first, until he reached a large area of thick undergrowth. Seeing no convenient means of circumvention, he hacked his way through thick forest for what seemed an eternity. Abruptly, the undergrowth came to a surprising end in a straight line of demarcation. He'd never seen anything like this in any of his numerous forays into the Northern Wilderness.

It was only a matter of minutes before he reached what he presumed was the previous residence of some form of intelligent life. What once had been dense foliage had been cleared in square configurations, as if they were rooms in a building. This was far more than merely one man's primitive campsite. Sam stood dumbfounded at the edge of a series of adjoining square and rectangular spaces, separated by "ghostly walls." His amazement peaked as he stepped closer to see that each of the walls in his proximity seemed to disappear and reappear with his movement. The walls were apparently not physical or tangible in the normal sense, but what were they? He stepped closer to one of the walls as it reappeared, and reached out his arm. The wall was ethereal and appeared to be composed of tiny light particles. His arm passed through effortlessly. He could not feel any increase in density or any resistance.

The walls resembled what one might see in a mansion on a large estate, tastefully adorned with artwork, and bordered by intricate woodcarving. As he walked around the periphery of the "structure," he noted that some of the walls were more distinct than others. Some were barely detectable and others were absent, leading him to speculate whether they lost visual structure and disappeared over time. There was one series of walls that was the most distinct of all. On either side of these were thin monolithic columns from which the walls appeared to project.

And then it hit him. The walls must be holograms of some sort! He remembered visiting a shop in a tourist town in the Midwest several years before that specialized in holograms, and these walls resembled the holographic images he'd marveled over at that time. The columns themselves looked somewhat like solar panels. He puzzled over why the residents would have left them behind, and wondered if they may have had to leave in a hurry. Sam walked from room to room, detecting the aromas of cooked food in one, the smell of pipe tobacco in another. In a room off to the side, he was surprised to see droppings from a variety of animal species that one wouldn't expect to see in the same location, inciting images in his mind's eye of a modern-day Noah, or perhaps a St. Francis.

Finding evidence of the trail of departure, he began to hike accordingly. He surged ahead for an hour before stopping to eat. Pulling some nuts and fruit from his pack, he sat down to catch his breath. He had eaten for a few minutes when his ears picked up the faint sound of a human voice on the breeze. Leaving the food on the ground, he cautiously moved in the direction of the sound, attempting to remain hidden. He heard the voice again, a low-pitched moan. Down an incline he saw a man lying on his side who appeared to be unconscious, with a wound on his temple. Approaching closer he recognized him. It was the man with the backpack from his dream.

Gillian was walking in a thick fog, groping into the darkness in front of him. He was despairing over an inability to see more than a few inches ahead, as well as over his failure in finding someone who was particularly vulnerable. He called out, but his words seemed to echo back at him. Suddenly he felt a vague pressure against the side of his head. As his focus gradually sharpened, he became aware that he was lying on his back, and detected the figure of a man reaching down and rubbing some sort of salve onto his left temple and forehead. Being initially frightened, he reached his arm up toward the figure.

"Easy... easy, I mean you no harm..." the man responded, while gently pushing Gil's arm back to his side. Sam Crowfeather reached back into his compact first aid kit and retrieved some gauze and a safety pin.

"That's some nasty cut you've got there..."

Gil's vision steadily cleared, and he perceived another figure behind his rescuer, also looking down at his wound. "Wh-...who are you guys?"

Sam wrapped the gauze around Gil's head. "It's just me. I'm Sam. What happened to you anyway?"

Gil began to sit up, and noticed that the other figure was suddenly gone. Sam helped him scoot over to a tree for support. "I dunno. The last thing I remember, I was lookin' up at the moon... I tripped over a tree root, I think it was... I must have hit my head on something and blacked out. My name's Gil, by the way."

Sam grabbed some bottled water from his pack and handed it to Gil. "Pleased to make your acquaintance. Here, you look kinda parched."

Gil drank the water, becoming suddenly aware of his thirst, and found Lottie entering into his thoughts. "Thank you. Hey, have you seen anyone else wandering around out here?"

Sam looked at him quizzically. "Blonde woman?"

Gil jerked forward. "Yes! Where did you see her?! Where is she?"

"Take it easy, okay? I haven't seen her."

Gil became defensive. "Whaddya mean?! You're not with the police, are you?!"

"Hey, c'mon, sit back down." Gil felt dizzy and Sam supported him until he resumed his position against the tree. "Look, number one, I'm not your enemy, number two, I guess you could say I'm a private investigator of sorts, number three, I've been told to keep on the look-out for you and a blonde woman. Beyond any of that, I'm not at liberty right now to divulge more information, other than to say that I'm looking for someone too. I'm a pilot. My plane's a few miles away and I can get you out of here eventually if you'd like. I'll tell you what. Why don't we hike together for a while, since we're both looking for someone?"

Gil thought about the offer and figured that it made sense. Safety in numbers. The guy didn't seem that threatening anyway, and Gil thought that by teaming up with Sam his chances of finding Lottie might improve. His curiosity as to who the other guy was, as well as how Sam would have known to be on the lookout for Lottie and himself were other compelling factors.

"Alright... so what direction should we go?"

Sam pointed to the northwest. "Thataway..."

· 16 ·

Elliot was in the doldrums. His followers had been keeping their distance from him lately. Previously they had been conditioned by a congenial presence, but were now confounded by an irascible tendency. He would snap at them for no obvious reason, and would then continue on as if nothing had happened, being utterly lacking in compunction. His Kingship remained unquestioned and unchallenged, but his behavior was becoming less and less benevolent, and more and more tyrannical. Tedium was an intolerable state of mind to Elliot. He was like Alexander the Great, who'd fallen into despair upon facing the horrifying prospect of having exhausted all existing fields of conquest.

Despair, however, was not a part of Elliot's emotional make-up. He was simply bored. He had reached the pinnacle of success in the world of "bricks and mortar" as he casually referred to it, and now had subdued the natural world under his heel. The moose had given him a run for his money, but were now coming around, thanks to the sly endeavor of his advisor, the reptile Balar. There seemed to be nothing left that would satisfy his voracious appetite for dominion. He desperately needed a new challenge.

Aside from all of that, there was another dawning personal issue. As Elliot's twilight years were approaching, he felt in need of a certain companionship. He would not tolerate a collaborator of any kind. The thought of a partner on an equal footing was repugnant to him. His absolute control must remain intact. His animal friends had been useful - yielding to his authority, and staving off any sense of social isolation. They were, however, limited in their ability to provide for another need, a craving he felt for communication and interaction with someone of his kind. As this desire came further into focus, it occurred to him that there just might be another frontier. That thought was foremost in the Monarch's mind as drowsiness overtook him after a long exhausting day of monotony and loneliness. Balar looked down from the tree upon him with a knowing gaze as Elliot crawled into his hammock at the edge of the forest and settled into a long, deep, dreamless, trance-like sleep.

He awoke in the morning feeling strangely as if he had just gone to sleep twenty minutes before. There was a rustling sound in the bushes and dry leaves several feet away into the woods. As the haze lifted from his eyes, he rolled over to see a figure emerging. It was a woman, looking disheveled, but oddly radiant after a night's sleep on the forest floor. He stood up and they faced each other with their mouths open and their eyes wide. For Elliot it was as if the heavens opened. He stared into her eyes and his mind seemed to explode with a sense of excitement and possibility. The very stones and shrubs seemed to speak out in concert with him. "Here at last is the embodiment of my aspirations. She shall be my cultural emissary... my goodwill ambassador ...my missionary to a world sunk in the depths of mediocrity, homogeneity and complacency..."

Lottie finally spoke. "Wh-...why you're the feller I done read about in that newspaper!!"

Elliot sighed. He had his work cut out for him.

Sam and Gil hiked for several hours, silently at first. Having been an outdoor enthusiast, it was refreshing for Gil to team up with someone like Sam. Nicolai had never been fond of long-distance hiking, which left Gil to do it on his own occasionally over the past fifteen years. He was now getting his long-distance chops back, and found it challenging to keep up with Sam, sometimes finding himself out of breath.

Gil became aware of a "freeing process" that began to take place in him. Dealing with Nick's manic phases had been a considerable burden, and he could feel it lifting. It even felt rather odd to be hanging with someone like Sam who seemed so functional and independent. At one point they stopped to eat and pondered their limited joint provisions. Gil was struck by how Sam seemed to be considerably less concerned about this predicament than he was. This prompted a conversation in which Sam spoke about survival techniques in the wild, and in particular about edible plants, many of which could be found in these northern woods. After eating, they continued through the forest.

Sensing that the ice had been broken, Sam spoke. "So tell me about your connection with the blonde woman..."

Gil felt uneasy. "Why do you want to know?"

"Well, if you're not comfortable talking about it, that's fine. I guess it's just the private eye in me. I'm curious to know what I'm dealing with here. At the very least I'd like to have a more detailed profile of her, so I know who I'm looking for. Aside from all that, we're kinda in this together now, don't you think?"

Gil thought about what Sam said and responded. "I guess you could say she's average to low average height, curly blonde hair, pretty in a 'salt of the earth' kind of way."

Sam could see in Gil's manner of description that he was quite fond of her.

"Her name's Lottie."

"Lottie... Lottie... now why does that sound so familiar?"

"Well you may have read about her in the news. She's the

one that just won the lottery."

"You mean the one that's missing?"

"Yeah, that's her." Gil realized at this point that he needed to cover his tracks.

"We met at that lottery affair at the Delmonica Ballroom. She was really upset. I was smitten with her from the beginning, and we decided on a lark to take off together, and headed north. We were stayin' at a cabin several miles from here, got in a fight and she ran off into the forest. I felt responsible for her and took off looking for her, and here I am..."

Sam suspected that there may be some details missing from Gil's account, recalling in particular his knee-jerk question as to whether Sam was with the police. He didn't press the point, however, in part due to a sudden distraction. "Do you hear that?"

Gil listened and could hear what sounded like classical music on the breeze. "What th-"

Sam put his finger to Gil's lips. "Shhhhhh."

He started moving slowly through the firs with as much stealth as he could muster. Gil followed behind. The music gradually gained in volume as they crept forward. They rounded a bend into a clearing and stopped dead in their tracks, falling to the ground behind some rhododendrons. Before them, about 50 yards away, was a herd of moose, but not just any herd of moose. The two rubbed their eyes in disbelief as they saw moose swaying and dancing to music that proceeded forth from a compact stereo in the middle of the clearing. Some of them appeared to be wearing clothing.

Sam surveyed the area and detected a large snake drooping down from a tree at the far end of the clearing. Though the moose hadn't seemed to detect their presence, the snake turned its head in their direction. Sam suddenly noticed that Gil was standing up, his wide eyes staring hypnotically at the snake. Gil began to walk toward the snake. Some kind of force seemed to be pulling him into the clearing. Sam grabbed him from behind and pulled him to the ground, wanting them to remain hidden from the moose, who could be dangerous if provoked. Gil struggled to get back to his feet, appearing to be in anything but his right mind. Feeling the sudden pull of the same force himself, Sam held onto Gil with all the strength he had. In an act of desperation he slapped Gil across the cheek. The spell broke and Gil looked back at him incredulously. Sam grabbed him by the arm. "C'mon, let's get out of here." Gil complied and they retreated a safe distance. On the way Sam picked up a piece of discarded cloth he'd seen lying on the ground. Catching his breath, he looked at the object of retrieval, a monogrammed towel. In the middle were the initials, E.T. This was the first definitive fruit of his investigation.

Gil looked at the initials, unaware of their significance. "Okay, you've got an 'aha' look on your face... whose initials are these?"

Sam kept silent, and Gil spoke again more insistently. "Look, I don't know what the hell just happened back there, but you said yourself we're in this together. I've told you my story, now it's time for you to fess up about yours!" For the second time Sam held a finger to Gil's lips.

"Shhhhhh, not so loud... Think about it, Gil, who else besides Lottie has been in the news lately?"

Gil thought back to the last newspaper he'd read at the convenience store with Nick and Lottie. He looked back at the towel. "Oh my God, Elliot Teagartin!"

· *17* ·

Elliot Teagartin could count on one hand the "close friends" he'd had in the course of his fifty-six years. His extended family members, who'd lost touch with him since the death of his parents, would question the use of the word "close," for as they would claim, relatives and acquaintances could get only so "close" to him. Friendship was not overly valuable to Elliot. Associations with others were mostly a matter of utility, a means to an end, and there were those over the years who'd felt slighted by Elliot and insisted that the man lacked the capacity for empathy, and was utterly devoid of compassionate regard for others.

Since he had stepped into the limelight at an early age, Elliot had been surrounded by an aura of mystery, which seemed to progressively enhance his celebrity status as the years rolled on. It was a wonder to his detractors that someone who spoke so often could be so ineffable, and conversely, that the more enigmatic he became, the more obsequious the public became in response. In speeches he imparted a sense of clever sophistication, but gave only scant, vague and often-contradictory clues to the inner man.

Elliot had generally exhibited a lack of personal interest in the opposite sex, but had been known to periodically indicate an admiration for what he described as "the woman's role" in binding the familial and cultural fabric of society, as well as a begrudging respect toward the collective power of women as "consumers" within the philosophical scheme of his theory of "Virtuous Consumerism." He was reviled by women's rights organizations, and by feminists in general, as being the pre-eminent chauvinists of the modern era. Nevertheless, as the years passed Elliot became all the more irresistible to countless western women due to a certain sexuality exuded by his dry wit and uncanny charm, and due to his physical appearance – taller than average, broad shoulders, the beginnings of middle-aged spread, slightly balding salt and pepper hair with streaks of gray, and a face with distinctive clean-shaven Anglo-Saxon features.

It was not unusual for men in particular to feel as if they'd been robbed of something in the aftermath of a conversation with Elliot. His penetrating eyes led those with whom he conversed to feel as if he knew them better than they knew themselves. In contrast, many women were enchanted through this dynamic, and Lottie Crump was no exception. Elliot's spell over her was profound, essentially due to a paternal quality he exercised, which addressed her desperate need for attention, after a lifetime of parental neglect. He made her feel secure, and his influence served as a healing balm toward that which she'd struggled against throughout her life – low self-esteem. She didn't fully understand his intentions toward her, but felt that his guidance was helping her to feel better about herself. Awareness was gradually dawning in her that, up to this point, her life had been lacking in something important – a sense of purpose. As such, she was ripe for the picking. She was a dry sponge, and held little within her in the way of resistance. She was putty in a guru's hands.

Aside from the charismatic presence of Elliot, and the holographic walls throughout the compound, Lottie was spellbound also by the animals in Elliot's company. She'd not previously had the opportunity to spend a lot of time around animals, but could sense intuitively that their behavior in attending to Elliot's every need was anything but natural. She'd never imagined that Dr. Doolittle was anything but a celluloid fantasy, but here he was in her midst.

Elliot could count on his devoted quadrupeds for most things, but for grooming Lottie in the acumen required for her mission as his philosophical surrogate, the task, by his design, was left to him, and him only. She did notice, however, that Balar was always there during her lessons from Elliot in such important skills as proper grammar and diction, appropriate manners, and good posture. She was vaguely uncomfortable with Balar's presence, and his eerie pulsing mode of telepathic communication. Balar's subtle influence over Elliot was confusing and somewhat disturbing to her as well, but she did not voice these reservations at first, being the creature of fear that she was. Besides, she was excited about what she was learning from Elliot, and after a week at the encampment, she felt blessed to spend some time with Elliot alone, or so she thought. They strolled together down a path on a ridge top near the settlement. Earlier in the day, Elliot had assisted the swans and peacocks in effecting a makeover for Lottie – a fresh change of clothing into a stylish evening gown, a manicure and pedicure, and the latest in cosmetics for her face.

Elliot was pleased with the results. "You look particularly beautiful tonight, my dear..."

Lottie blushed. "Thank you..." She recovered her composure and summoned the courage to satisfy her curiosity. "Mr. Teagartin, can I ask you somethin'?"

Elliot corrected her. "Tsk, tsk, tsk, now what would be a better means of expressing that, hmmm?"

Lottie swallowed and took a deep breath. "Ummm... may I ask you a question?"

"Very good! Very good, my dear. Now ask to your heart's

content... ask away!"

"Okay...what made you wanna, er, I mean, umm, what motivated you to come out here to the boonies -er, uh... the wilderness?"

Elliot smiled. He could discern that she was exercising a genuine attempt at upgrading her erudition, and was confident that, in time, she would transcend her appalling cultural beginnings.

"Have you ever heard of Julius Caesar, Letitia, dear heart?"

Lottie shook her head.

"Well, he was a great Roman Emperor, known for saying, 'I came, I saw, I conquered'..." Elliot lapsed into a reflective mode, staring off into the distance. He sat down on a fallen oak tree beside the path. "There was simply nothing left for me there, you understand... I felt in need of a 'new beginning,' shall we say, and I'd run into a bit of a problem." Suddenly, a certain reptile reminded Elliot that he was offering too much information. "Oh well... suffice it to say that I was intrigued by the prospect of this unbridled frontier, and felt a desire to unleash a taming influence upon it, as one might with a wild stallion."

Lottie was puzzled. "But what was wrong with it the way it was? I mean, after all, didn't the Good Lord make it that way?"

Elliot smiled again. His protégé was coming along, but still had a ways to go.

"Don't misunderstand me, my precious... I wouldn't suggest that there was something evil here, or anywhere, for that matter." He looked up at Balar hanging down from a poplar branch. "No... there is only ignorance, my dear... only ignorance."

Sam and Gil pressed onward, spending the night in an abandoned hunter's cabin that they had discovered. As they neared the outskirts of Elliot's current encampment the following day, they had enough provisions for one meal, and a meager one at that. They approached the crest of a hill that would overlook the convergence of the two streams Sam had seen from the air. This is where he presumed they'd find Elliot and company. They perched themselves on a rocky outgrowth at the hilltop and Sam retrieved the binoculars from his pack. He perused the area for a few minutes and then sat back, shaking his head.

Gil looked imploringly at him. "What?!"

Sam handed him the binoculars. "Look for yourself... that certainly isn't normal behavior down there. Under natural circumstances those wolves would be chasing and eating those deer, but there they are, standing side by side."

Gil focused the instrument and surveyed the area himself. "I see what you mean... what are those weird things that keep disappearing?"

"I don't know for sure, but I think they're holograms," came Sam's reply.

Gil looked back at him and shook his head. "Unbelievable! So, what now?"

Sam thought about how much information he should divulge at this point. "Well, I set out on this part of the mission with one goal, to determine whether Teagartin is alive. In order to establish that, I have to see him. At best we've got four hours of daylight left. Let's cut a wide swath around the area and see what we can find. With any luck we may see him, and then we can return to the cabin for the night."

Gil looked at Sam and nodded his assent. He was growing more apprehensive each day at not having found Lottie, and was beginning to imagine the worst. Sam was obviously skilled in the business in which he was currently engaged, and if they parted ways at this point Gil feared that he would likely get lost in the wilderness without sufficient means of survival. They stopped at several points of observation over the next few hours, seeing various animals, but no humans. Finally they reached a high point overlooking a ridge top, and climbed a large beech tree for a better view. Sam once again retrieved the binoculars. In the distance beyond the ridge he could see smoke rising and speculated that perhaps a meal was being prepared. He fixed the lenses on the ridge top and moved them slowly along its course until he suddenly detected movement. It was a human figure.

"Bingo... there he is." Sam kept the binoculars fixed upon what appeared to be the man from the dossier. He waited until he came back into view from behind some trees. After further observation he was certain that it was Elliot. "Wait... there's someone else." Elliot appeared to be walking with a woman. He gave the binoculars to Gil, and pointed downward. "Look down there... could that be her?"

Gil focused the lenses and peered through the instrument at the ridge top until he saw the two humans. He followed their course as they walked down the path. "Well, I'll be damned!" He could hardly believe his eyes and handed the binoculars back to Sam.

Sam started to get impatient. "Well?!?"

Gil looked back at him wide-eyed. "It's her all right... it's her walking down that path with Elliot Teagartin!"

Sam sat back, relieved that he'd finally found the prize, but apprehensive about what he was about to suggest to his hiking companion. "Okay... listen, we've got one small meal left. I've seen Elliot and you've found Lottie. She appears to be safe for now, right? I say we head back to the cabin and eat. We'll spend another night there, and then tomorrow we'll hike back to the plane."

Gil suddenly protested. "Now, wait a minute!"

Sam interrupted. "Look, I'm late in reporting back to the guy who hired me for this investigation. I wasn't counting on this trip taking as long as it did. I promise you we'll come back within another week. I've got more work to do here, and I could use the company. But right now we've got to face facts, Gil. We're about out of food, and despite what I said about survival techniques, I'd rather use them some other time when I have no choice. We'll come back in another week with adequate provisions and perhaps the means to protect ourselves, if necessary."

Gil was uneasy about this last point. "What do you mean by that?"

"I mean that there's something not right going on down there, something dark, and I don't intend to go back without a way to protect myself, in case it becomes necessary."

Gil decided that he didn't want more details. He sat back and tried to digest all that he'd just seen and heard. His gut told him that Sam was probably right. He looked Sam in the eye, and had to admit to himself that Sam hadn't given him any reason to doubt his intentions. Besides that, he felt like Daffy Duck staring down the Lone Ranger. He obviously needed Sam more than Sam needed him. He took a deep breath and sighed.

"All right, kemosabe, let's go..."

· 18 ·

It took most of the following day to get to the plane. Having not eaten all day, the two were exhausted and irritable as they neared the landing site. Gil had thereby picked a lousy moment to satisfy a mounting curiosity.

"So, who was that guy who was with you when we met up?" Sam was not in the mood for a conversation, and could only think about the emergency food rations back in the plane.

"I doubt you'd believe me if I told you."

Gil was stubbornly insistent. "Try me!"

"Look... just let me eat something first, and on the way back I'll try and explain."

They reached the plane and Sam fetched some water and freeze-dried cereal and fruit. He prepared the food and they ate. Gil marveled at what a powerful force hunger could be. Though he was thankful for the food, he tended to be particular about his diet, and would never let such devitalized material pass his lips under normal circumstances.

The sky above them looked ominous. A storm front appeared to be moving in. They got strapped into the plane, and Sam started the engine. A strong wind was beginning to howl through the flatland, which aided the takeoff, lifting the plane into the air effortlessly. Once aloft, the first few hours were relatively peaceful, with only some mild turbulence here and there. This was Gil's first plane flight in such a small plane, and he looked out the window in awe at the vast wilderness below, while the last moments of daylight gradually waned. He asked about restroom facilities and Sam pointed to a stall in the back of the plane.

After relieving himself, Gil stepped out and took a few steps before being suddenly thrown onto the floor in the mid-section. Heavy turbulence gripped the plane as loud thunder and cracks of lightning could be heard. Gil struggled to get back on his feet to no avail, as the plane jerked up and down, beset by instantaneous shifts in altitude. In the cockpit Sam struggled to remain in his seat as the plane violently shifted and heavy rain crashed onto the front windshield. Back in the mid-section, Gil was repeatedly thrown around the plane and finally collided with the side of one of the four passenger seats. As the plane continued to shake, he looked up incredulously to see a bearded man asleep in the left front aisle seat. The plane jerked downward and the Witness opened his eyes. He looked around, quickly sensing the circumstances, and lifted his right hand into the air. The squall ceased in an instant and peace was restored. The Witness closed his eyes again. Gil rolled over onto his stomach and arose to his feet to find that the left front aisle seat was empty.

Sam entered the mid-section after having stabilized the plane and switched on the autopilot. He found Gil standing awkwardly, looking awe-stricken. "Are you all right? I thought we were goin' down there for a minute..."

Gil was barely able to speak. He pointed at the seat. "He... he...."

Sam took him by the arm, led him to a seat in the cockpit, and sat down to resume the controls. A half-minute passed and Sam looked over at Gil. His eyes were wide, as if he was still caught in the previous moment. Sam broke the silence. "Did you see someone?"

Gil continued to be speechless.

"Was it the guy you saw when we met?"

Gil pondered the question and looked excitedly over at Sam. "Yes! It was him... he stopped the storm... he just reached up and stopped it!"

Sam smiled. "There... now you know as much about him as I do."

Sam and Gil had been back in the city for a few days. They'd shared a cab from the airport and had agreed to get in touch with each other after the better part of a week. Sam sat at his kitchen table working on a letter to Father Dominic. This was to be his last responsibility to the clergyman. His intention was to wash his hands of any further investigative work through this correspondence. He recalled his original feeling when reading the dossier – that Elliot appeared to be lilywhite compared to other seamy targets of Fr. Dominic's investigations. The irony was that Teagartin might well turn out to be the spookiest character of them all.

On the other hand, Sam was the prototypical doubting Thomas. It was not in his nature to trust fully in a hunch, or even in his own intuition. He had to put his fingers in the wounds. He must see for himself. It was still possible that everything he'd seen so far was above board, despite his doubts. From here on out he wished to pursue the matter without the Priest, for it had become personal to him. He'd grown progressively wearier over the years of feeling bifurcated between his European and Native American roots, and their sharply contrasting values. This man Elliot Teagartin somehow struck at the heart of this struggle for Sam. He needed to find out who Elliot "was," and through doing so, he hoped to be able once and for all to make a choice about who Sam Crowfeather "is." He put down his pen and sat back to review what he had written:

> Fr. Dominic,
>
> Teagartin is alive and living in the Northern Woods. Enclosed is a towel found near his current settlement. Note the initials. Sorry about the missed deadline. It took longer to locate him than expected. Some of the tabloid accounts are true – wild animals tamed, tracts of wilderness transformed into villages, etc. Don't know why you & your associates want to find this guy, but believe me, your best decision would be to walk away from this, and not look back, you know? Pillars of salt and all that. I'm not being cute or making a joke here – there's something twisted about this situation, and you're too good a man to get soiled by this thing. You deserve better. This is where our business association ends. I don't care if I get paid for this one – consider it a gift for all of the business you've sent my way over the years. I'm not getting any younger, and I've lost the stomach for this kind of work. All the best to you. I hope you find what you're looking for.
>
> Sam

Yep, this'll do, Sam thought. Direct and to the point, and yet personal at the same time. He and Fr. Dominic had shared some good times together, and he felt he owed him at least this much. The two shared an interest in Orthodox Christian Monasticism, and had attended services together at a monastery on several occasions. They had even tentatively planned on going to Mt. Athos together at one point, and Sam wondered what had become of those mutual yearnings. He put the letter and towel in a cardboard package and took off for the post office.

When he returned he found a message on his machine from Gil asking him to meet him for dinner at a Mexican restaurant on the South Side. He had something important to discuss with him.

"Good! Good." Sam thought. Perhaps he wouldn't have to cajole it out of him after all. He'd become fond of Gil and was looking forward to hiking up north with him again, but before this was going to happen, Sam needed the truth. He was fairly certain that something was missing from the skimpy account Gil offered as to how he wound up in the Northern Wilderness. Perhaps tonight, he hoped, the light would shine fully on his newfound friend. Perhaps tonight Gil would come out of the shadows.

Gil moved slowly through traffic to the south side of town in his old beat-up Jeep. He felt relieved. For a couple of days he'd been at the apartment that he and Nick had shared for the past seven years, and it had depressed him. The dwelling was full of memorabilia from a life he'd abandoned, and utterly devoid of anything that would bring focus to the vague new life he'd chosen. He missed Lottie terribly, and feared that he may have lost her to a cunning aristocrat. He also wondered what had happened to Nick, and suspected that being in the apartment was connected with a few bad dreams he'd suffered since coming back. Both nightmares were about the kidnapping, and both had left him in a cold sweat, feeling guilty about Nick's fate. If only he had refused to go along with the insane idea.

If only. But then he reminded himself that otherwise he might have never met Lottie. The good news was that, as near as he could tell, he and Nick had not been implicated in any kind of foul play surrounding the disappearance of Lottie. He'd gone to the local library and reviewed all of the recent newspapers. From what he could gather, the authorities were rather clueless about the missing lottery queen. There were plenty of suspicions, but no evidence to support them. He could hardly believe it. They'd actually pulled it off. There had been no grand payoff in the way of ransom, but that was all the more comforting as far as he was concerned. If any part of the crazy scheme had landed them in prison, it would have involved his loony music partner trying to extract ransom from Lottie's stoned father.

There were two points of bad news. The first was that eviction proceedings were being initiated on the apartment. Gil had found a notice on the door giving them thirty days to vacate, so he had loaded up what little he wanted from the apartment in the Jeep, not intending to ever return. The second bit of bad news involved a newspaper article he'd found about the death of Lottie's father. He imagined that he might wind up being the one to inform Lottie of this when they met up again, if they ever met up again. As for tonight, he planned to come clean. He needed Sam's help to find out what happened to Nick. He also needed a place to stay, and had a hunch that Sam would accommodate him. Tonight he'd level with Sam. Tonight he'd get that whole nasty mess off of his chest.

· 19 ·

Balar looked down upon the moose, his reptilian eyes dripping with delight. It had taken only a token degree of persuasion to get them to keep turning the dial... turning the dial to forbidden stations where exotic notions of good and evil would gain entrance to their ears. Over the past week the moose had descended precariously down one long slippery slope from the sublime to the ridiculous, from the summit of the language of the soul to the depths of the auditory abyss. And ohhh how sensuous were the sounds that echoed up out of that abyss! This was despite the moose's better nature which would have them clinging to Johann Sebastian and George Frederick with all their heart, mind and soul. They had "progressed." They were "coming along well" as Elliot would say.

And what had been the tricks up Balar's slimy sleeve? Well, Balar is a secretive creature. Suffice it to say that he had casually insinuated a few tidbits into their consciousness which awakened tendencies that were already there lying dormant, waiting for the flip of a switch. Pass the buck and follow the herd... pass the buck and follow the herd... It took one moose to turn the dial, and another to respond instinctually and provocatively to the new sound. When other moose looked disapprovingly upon the provocateur, he would point to the one who turned the dial as if to say, "She made me do it!" And, by the time the entire herd had tuned into those sounds, the seeds had been planted. There was no turning back. They had been cast out, and Mozart stood with a golden spear at the gates baring their return.

Sadly, as if to ensure their survival, before long they were all doing it. They were all provocateurs marching to the beat like children following the Pied Piper. After all, who wants to stand alone and be different? The isolation and loneliness would be unbearable. Balar surveyed his endeavors as his forked tongue slid repetitively out of his mouth and back in again.

"Life is indeed a cabaret," he declared, with his telepathic buzz. The moose stood in a row on the mock stage rehearsing their act. They all had multi-colored day-glo wigs hanging from their antlers, pasties swinging from their hind ends, and peek-a-boo clothing draped across their abdomens. They finished one performance, resumed their positions, and waited for Balar's cue. "OKAY... LET'S HEAR IT AGAIN FROM THE TOP!"

Up there so loosy-goosy...
You sexy moosey moosey...
You break my heart, you hurt my pride...
You keep me beggin... for another ride...

On your loopy whoopee train...
You won't hear me complain...
I'd follow you anywhere...
In the snow, in the sleet or the rain...

Balar shrewdly smiled down once again upon his work of creation to see that it was good... it was useful... it would fulfill his purposes. Tomorrow the moose would debut before an audience comprised of Elliot and his vast company of recruits. And who knows what may happen after that? The future was limitless.

"Broadway, here we come!"

Lottie Crump lay down for a night's rest after a long exhausting day of training with Elliot, who'd been edgy and distracted all day. He was apprehensive about the evening's scheduled entertainment, a bawdy Las Vegas-type floorshow from the moose. Though Lottie and the animals whole-heartedly enjoyed the performance, Elliot was visibly annoyed. The best he could do was clap politely at the curtain call before going off by himself to brood. He considered the whole affair to be nothing short of a tawdry entertainment. Sensing that he may have paid a dear price for trusting in Balar's handling of this delicate project, he especially was concerned about the effect such a crass display may have upon the impressionable Letitia, whom he was grooming to be his right arm in the unseen campaign against this kind of cultural vapidity.

However, he was, as usual, at a loss to address the issue directly, due to the tenuous nature of the relationship between Balar and himself. His association with the snake went back quite a ways, beginning at the time just before Elliot had first stepped onto the world stage as a young man. Elliot's vulnerabilities were generally unknown by the rest of the world, and when in the past he'd felt his ambition stifled, he could always count on exercising the fail safe option of slipping into the shadows and receiving the counsel from his serpentine advisor that would lead to the removal of the obstacle to his aims, either through Elliot's action, or through a mysterious intervention from Balar himself. As a result, Balar would periodically assert that Elliot was beholden to him, which struck at the core of Elliot's uneasiness about the association. Deep down Elliot suspected that he needed Balar, and he was never able to be comfortable or at peace with the association due to the disconcerting fact that Balar was the only individual in Elliot's life that he could not control. Indeed, Elliot himself at times felt vaguely controlled by Balar.

Though Lottie was unaware of this background between her illustrious teacher and the seemingly omnipresent reptile, she could sense that Elliot was torn in two directions by the relationship, one of dependence and another of distrust. When she attempted in the course of the day to question Elliot as to why he let the snake "...tell him what to do..." as she put it, she'd hit a raw nerve. Elliot flew into a rage.

"YOU, MY DEAR, ARE VENTURING INTO TERRITORY THAT IS NOT YOURS TO TREAD!!" She suspected that he may have "man-handled" her at that point, had it not been for Balar himself, who pulled him back through that eerie supernatural force that he exercised over those in his midst. Instead, Elliot stormed off into the forest to regain his composure, and later returned, acting as if nothing had happened. Needless to say, Lottie had been frightened out of her wits by such uncharacteristic behavior from Elliot, and it required unwinding before the dancing moose to calm her nerves.

Now she drifted off to sleep and found herself walking down a thoroughfare toward a marble building with Roman columns and a funeral hearse parked at the front curb. Standing in the front entryway was the Witness, looking at her as if he was expecting her. He accompanied her into the building where they entered the back of a chapel and walked between empty pews to the front, toward a coffin that lay elevated on wheels. Lottie felt afraid and yet compelled to look into the coffin. The body looked familiar. As she focused more upon the reclining figure, she gasped to realize that it was her father. Her jaw dropped and she shook her head slowly from side to side. She turned to the Witness as if to ask, "What happened?" She couldn't cry, but felt suspended in disbelief. She and the Witness embraced and he spoke quietly into her ear.

"The flames approached from either side until they met in the middle. It was his time. I thought you should know..." She let go to see that the Witness was holding a rose and handing it to her. She took the rose and placed it in the coffin with Daddy, looking at her father for the last time in this life before turning to leave with the Witness. They walked down the boulevard together.

She ended her silence. "I never knew what to do for him... I always felt helpless. It's the same way with Mr. Teagartin! I don't know what to do..."

The Witness looked at her with concern. "Your situation now is dangerous. You needn't say anything to him, the less you say, the better. Things are not what they seem. But don't worry, help is on the way..."

They kept walking and noticed flashing red lights and a bar dropping at a railroad crossing. They approached and stopped before the passing freight train. It roared loudly down the tracks until Lottie was swallowed whole by the sound. Thunder rumbled above her as she awoke in her hammock, and then the tears came, streaming down her face with the soft rain. She sat up and wept quietly with her face in her hands, like she often did as a little girl. Memories began to flood through her consciousness as she whispered, "My Daddy's gone... he done left me all by my lonesome... one last time..."

Father Dominic read the letter from Sam over and over while he ingested glass after glass of red wine. It was not the result he'd hoped for. He kept reading the letter, but it didn't change to suit him. It kept repeating the same thing. He trusted Sam. Sam had never steered him wrong. The monogrammed towel seemed superfluous. He knew that if Sam reported that Teagartin was alive, he could count on Teagartin being alive. He'd never had the courage to tell him to his face, but he admired and envied Sam. Sam didn't need a clerical collar to fortify his spiritual aspirations.

He just naturally gravitated toward them without the need of an institutional seal.

The forlorn clergyman put the letter down and let the truth begin to sink into his consciousness. He had hoped that Elliot was dead, and the Church could go forward with its idiotic scheme of canonizing their "new-found nature mystic." That way, at least a holding pattern could be established for a while, and perhaps in the meantime some kind of sanity, whatever it may be, could rise above the clamor of the Church's continuous drive to be "relevant."

But alas, Teagartin was alive, and now, as it had time and time again, the bar would be lowered once more. He shuddered to think of what the next preposterous idea may be that his superiors would conjure up out of the voodoo cauldron into which they were sinking. They'd already ushered in an era of drive-in liturgical rites and coin-operated video confessionals. He stared into an ominous future and could sense that a breaking point was approaching. Sooner or later he would have no choice but to throw in the towel, as frightening as it seemed. He hoped that he still had a shred of dignity left. He hoped that his conscience would demand no less.

· 20 ·

Calen Foster and Sam Crowfeather sat in a booth at a midtown diner on a busy city avenue. A few blocks in one direction was the central precinct of the Metropolitan Police, and about as many blocks the other way was the high rise where the Tribune had its offices, two formidable institutions of the contemporary era, both engaged in the business of gathering information through processes of investigation.

The relationship between the various forms of media and the various branches of law enforcement can, at times, be tenuous, and even downright testy. Their aims in gathering information, while not at odds by definition, can sometimes be at cross purposes, for the one has as its goal to inform the public, while the other's end revolves around ensuring that laws aren't breached. The former generally seeks to make information known, while the latter often endeavors to keep information secret.

And then there are characters like Sam Crowfeather, private investigators who track down information in the interests of private parties who either aim to shine a light, or to impose darkness at all costs. In this instance, however, Sam's desire was of a more lofty nature. He was digging for, and disseminating information in order to seek "truth," both for his own personal edification, and increasingly for the sake of serving that force in the universe that was greater than himself, or any one man or institution, that supreme benevolence to which he felt himself accountable. For the truth-seeker, truth itself holds inherent value, but for many in the contemporary era, truth is becoming irrelevant. The search for truth has become discarded by many amid the intellectual din of relativism, and the stifling pathos of consumerism. The roots of relativism stretch back to the ancient world. "What is truth?" asked Pontius Pilate. Though often lacking in spiritual significance, "information," as opposed to "truth," was the currency that had played a large part in toppling an American Presidency only seven short years ago, and it was information that would eventually be a factor in the demise of our anti-hero, Elliot Teagartin.

"He's out there, all right... I haven't entirely figured out yet what the nature is of the situation, but I can tell you that it's weird. A lot of the tabloid accounts are accurate: strange animal behavior, holographic walls... a veritable 'settlement' with most of the trappings of civilization, without the bricks and mortar."

"Well... first of all," Cale interjected, "you have actually seen Teagartin himself, correct?"

"Yes... from a distance through binoculars. It was definitely him."

"Any other humans?"

Sam thought quickly and concluded that he'd better keep Lottie under wraps.

"I haven't gotten close enough yet to ascertain that, but I've certainly seen a lot of animals!"

"Tell me, then, about the strange animal behavior."

"Well, the one odd thing I've noticed repeatedly is how the carnivores and the animals they'd normally hunt for food are hanging out together as if the predator-prey relationship doesn't apply. Teagartin seems to have acclimated the animals to exotic, gourmet-type fare, the kind of diet that some humans couldn't tolerate."

"Holographic walls?!?"

"Well... that's what they appear to me to be." And so on, and so forth. Sam gave Cale as much information as he felt comfortable imparting, including a general sense of where the current encampment is from the vantage point of Sunnyvale. "Look for a large pool of water where two streams converge, northwest of town about 10 miles. I would suggest hiring a guide."

"Tell me more."

"Well, you're going on horseback, right?"

"Hopefully."

"It would cost you some money, probably a daily fee, but it would be well worth it to head out with someone who knows the area, familiar with the terrain."

"Anyone you would suggest?"

"There's an old guy in Sunnyvale I know. He used to hang out with the Beat Poets in the city during the '50s, makes a living collecting ginseng, wild mushrooms and other things I won't mention. He's been doing that for 20 years or more in the forests around town. A little rough around the edges, but he'll get you there and back. I don't recall what his full name is, but he goes by 'Duffy.' Everyone in Sunnyvale knows him. Most folks stay away from him, but his bark's worse than his bite."

Cale put down his pen. "I can't thank you enough, Sam. Like I said before, I'm afraid I don't have anything to offer in return right now, I guess I'll just have to owe you one."

"Actually, you do have something to offer. If you don't mind, I'd like to cash in on that favor right now."

Cale was surprised. "Okay. Go on..."

"You've still got some contacts at the precinct down the street, right?"

"Yeah, some of the same ones from a few years back, why?"

"I need to find out what happened to someone, no questions asked, a guy by the name of, uhhh... hold on..." Sam pulled a piece of paper from his shirt pocket. "Nicolai Zagorski, last seen two weeks ago in a cabin about 15 miles northeast of Sunnyvale." Sam handed the paper to Cale. "We hope that he was picked up by the police and medics unharmed. He had a shoulder wound, and may have been carrying a firearm. That's all I know."

Cale finished writing down Sam's information. "Well, I can't promise anything, but I'll see what I can find out. You heading back to the wilderness soon?"

"In a few days. Can you have the information for me by then?"

Cale took another sip of coffee and looked out the window. "It's a tall order, but I'll see what I can do..."

After meeting with Cale, Sam left his vehicle in the parking lot and took a walk around the city. His original intent was to clear his head and gain some perspective over the events of the past few months. He looked at the tall buildings, the vehicles rushing through the streets, and the people moving about on the sidewalk. Walking by stairwells leading to the subways, he could feel the rumble of all of the movement – so many people going in a multitude of directions. The more he walked, the more disoriented he became, until he gave up on gaining clarity and returned to his vehicle.

Having returned home, Sam laid his head down for the night late into the evening and fell into a deep sleep, finding himself once again in the company of the Witness. They flew far above the world in the earth's atmosphere in a manner incomprehensible to him. Below him was a breathtaking view of clouds stretched out as far as he could see. He assumed that he must be dreaming, and yet felt peace, comfort, and protection in the ineffable embrace of the Witness, who carried him below the clouds to a vista that was beyond imagination in its majesty. "Do you see that, Sam? Below you is the earth in its primordial state."

The beauty of what Sam beheld was overwhelming to his senses – virgin forests, pristine snow-capped mountains, pure cascading water, colors so intense that it was all he could do to hold his gaze. He wept and shook his head. "What happened?!?"

"Well, we were fruitful and multiplied. To that extent we were obedient. Beyond that some would contend that the results of our multiplication were catastrophic. But to dwell excessively on the past is dubious in its fruitfulness." The Witness then swept Sam back to contemporary earth, where he witnessed large urban infrastructures mixed in with natural environments. There was a haze in the atmosphere that hovered above the cities, but there were still blue skies in the less developed areas. Much of the forested earth had been replaced by agrarian landscapes, but areas remained in which natural ecosystems existed. "Earlier today in your walk around the city, you couldn't see the forest for the trees, as they say. It looks quite different from up here doesn't it?"

"Yes it does. It feels as if there is reason for hope."

"Yes. As long as this earth is here, there will always be reason for hope. Yours is a great soul, Sam, and you can be of great service to your fellow man as he is now, if you so choose. I know I warned against dwelling on the past, but please don't misunderstand me. We must learn the lessons of the past, but only in order to concentrate on the present and future of man on this planet with the benefit of wisdom gleaned from the mistakes as well as the triumphs of the past. There is renewal that is occurring and further renewal that needs to happen on the earthly plain, but there is work to be done on the unseen level as well, and this is where I suspect that you will primarily operate, in accordance with the gifts granted you."

Then the Witness took Sam beyond the earthly sphere to a realm that couldn't be easily described, if at all, where all was bliss. A light shined that he couldn't behold due to its intense brightness. The joy Sam felt overflowed to the point that he shed a veritable waterfall of grateful tears. He was unable to speak. "This is the ultimate goal, Sam. Our earthly endeavor is not an end in itself, but is expended in the hope of basking in the glow of the Uncreated Light."

The Witness returned Sam gently to the confines of his mortal body. He awoke that morning with vivid memories, and a melancholy that was to grip his consciousness throughout the day. He knew not why he was sad, but was strangely at peace with the mystery.

· 21 ·

A week had gone by and the wilderness guide extraordinaire
had kept to his word. Gil was on his way to the precinct
headquarters of the Metropolitan Police, where he had been
instructed by Sam to pick him up. From there they'd be heading
to the airport for another trip to the Northern Wilderness. Gil
was anticipating that Sam might have some news for him. Sam
had arranged to meet Cale Foster at the precinct that morning,
and was aware that Cale's connection would be going out on a limb
to get such confidential information regarding the fate of Nicolai.
"Don't expect too much," Sam had warned Gil before heading
to the precinct in a cab. Gil's Jeep carried all the materials and
provisions they'd need for an extended foray into the forest. This
morning's detective work was their last order of business before
their departure. It had taken a combination of firm resolve from
Gil and some prodding by Sam to get the truth completely out in
the open the other night. And now, the only other person who
knew about the kidnapping aside from Nick and Lottie was Sam
Crowfeather.

If Gil had been reticent at all, it was due to the risk inherent
in divulging such sensitive information. Sam could turn them in to
the police if he was so inclined, but the gamble turned out in Gil's

favor. Sam showed no sign of betraying the secret. This was, as Gil assumed, partly due to the influence of the Witness, who for mysterious reasons was keeping an eye out for the welfare of Lottie and Gil. Beyond that, Sam had to have noticed his contrition over having absconded with Lottie against her will, and that was apparently enough to satisfy his need to have matters put right again. Gil was not only repentant, but thankful, for he'd found a stable friend in Sam, someone with a kind of virtue he'd rarely seen in others, and to boot, he was getting the services not only of a wilderness guide, but also of a private eye free of charge. He pulled into the precinct parking lot, seeing Sam walking through the lot toward the Jeep. Sam got in and they pulled out into traffic toward the airport expressway.

"He couldn't give me anything but a verbal report, but I'll tell you what I know. I was able to dash off some notes. Let's see..." Sam flipped back through his steno pad to the beginning. "An anonymous tip was called in to the local authorities in Sunnyvale... an ambulance and police cruiser were dispatched to the scene... your friend was arrested and taken to a local hospital, after they found him staggering down a country road with a gunshot wound... he was carrying a firearm and apparently got one shot off before collapsing. Lucky for him, the reports indicate that the police didn't fire back in response. There's more good news... your partner must have recovered enough from the wound to be moved. The bad news is that he must have gone off the deep end... he's now on a locked ward in a State Institution, but which one exactly he didn't say, probably because he didn't know himself." Sam double-checked his notes. "Looks like that's all I was able to get."

Gil let the information sink in for a moment before speaking. "Thank you, Sam. It's more than enough info, and I appreciate your efforts. What I wanted to know more than anything is that Nick is safe and being looked after. As for where he wound up, well... it may be unfortunate, but it was inevitable. Nick had been heading in that direction for as long as I've known him... I was able to keep him on the straight and narrow for just so long before I got dragged into the proverbial floodwater with him. I guess I just couldn't hold my finger in the dyke any longer."

The Chosen One had been marginalized. Previously his stature had been swiftly elevated through being the one among the moose selected to retrieve the "sacred boombox," and now he had been knocked off that pedestal with a comparable rapidity.

"Turn back!" he implored them, "Turn back before it's too late!" His brothers and sisters had fallen to the auditory idol, and they found his "voice in the wilderness routine" annoying, that is, when they actually heard it, being distracted as they were most of the time by the increasingly worldly sounds that oozed forth from the beast in the clearing. In his isolation, the Chosen One's psyche vacillated between feelings of aching loneliness, and the resolve that arises from a sense of "calling," from a revelatory nudge, an inducement from a higher intelligence. He had encountered the Witness in the forest, whose support strengthened his sense of mission against the hopelessness and despair that often overwhelmed him. The Witness praised his efforts and emboldened him for the unseen warfare that he waged for the hearts, minds and souls of his fellow moose against the designs of the reptile Balar.

The Chosen One was the only one among the moose who questioned whether Elliot Teagartin's influence was directed in the best interest of the herd, and took it upon himself to carry forward the mischievous behavior toward Elliot and his entourage that his brothers and sisters had long since abandoned. Despite being castigated by the rest, he spoke for the herd as if their previous spirit of solidarity continued into the present. He tiptoed into Elliot's encampment under the cover of night to deliver a message.

Circling his way around to the King's Bed Chamber, he left the note for Elliot, who was preparing for a night's sleep. The Chosen One escaped into the forest not a moment too soon, as the King approached. Elliot removed his bathrobe, hung it on a branch, and turned to lie down, noticing that a piece of paper lay in the center depression of the hammock. He picked it up and threw it down in a fit of exasperation.

"Damnation!" There on the edge of the bed lay the message in big bold black letters: "WE KNOW WHO YOU ARE."

Lottie was asleep... or was she awake? She couldn't tell which. She heard voices, an angry contentious rant, alternating with an arrogant glib response. She kept turning in different directions to ascertain the sources, but couldn't see anything, she could only hear...

"...I would have appreciated you asking for my ideas regarding the situation!"

"You would do best not to expect such things from me, I will do as I wish..."

"It was a shameless vulgar display, and it doesn't appear to have worked!"

"It has been more than efficacious, you're just upset because your pathetic sense of propriety has been violated."

"OH, SO IT HAS WORKED, HAS IT?!? THEN HOW DO YOU EXPLAIN THIS??" (The vague sound of rustling paper... uproarious telepathic laughter.)

"So... just who do you think you are, Mr. Teagartin?" (more buzzing laughter)

"And just what do you mean by that?!"

"You would do well to remember who is in control here..."

Lottie awoke in her hammock and realized who the participants were in the conversation. She did her best to ignore the rest of what was being said as she quietly slipped into some clothes and out into the forest, carrying her footwear. She found a fallen tree and sat down to put on her shoes. She'd grown increasingly anxious over the past several days, and was no longer comfortable in the compound. Her old foe, fear, was back in full force. It was more than she could bear to wake up to the sounds of the Prince and the snake verbally sparring with each other, and she stood up and walked further into the forest away from the "virtual village." She longed to be somewhere out of the elements where the walls were solid, but could see nothing but wilderness in all directions.

Lottie had been thinking a lot about Gil lately since her situation at the encampment had turned sour. She missed him terribly, and for the first time since she escaped into the forest weeks ago, she allowed herself to ponder what may have happened when that gun went off. The thought that he may have been killed brought tears to her eyes. Unfortunately, she had no idea whether she'd ever see Gil again, and now saw no point in continuing to think about it. She had more pressing concerns, and said goodbye to Gil quietly while saying a prayer that one day she'd see him again.

"But now... what about what's happening right now?" she asked quietly, becoming vaguely aware that she was expecting someone else to jump in and save the day. No one answered. Lottie walked for a few more hours, immersed in thought. As the distance from Elliot's enclave increased, she felt all the more relaxed and began to contemplate all that had transpired over the past few weeks. "Why am I afraid now?" she asked herself internally. This was an important step for Lottie, perhaps the first time that she had reflected upon herself in such a manner. She'd learned this from the Witness, who'd advised her to close her eyes, take a deep breath, and ask herself that question when she was distraught – "Why am I afraid?" The answer came. Her mentor had been drinking excessively. He was morphing from a parent into a tyrant. She had become dependent upon Elliot, and this change in him was frightening to her, and all too familiar. For years she'd watched her father gradually disintegrate from drink. It appeared to be her pattern to seek parental support from alcoholics.

And then it was as if a new concept had been introduced to her. "I need to learn to stand on my own two feet!" she thought to herself as she continued to walk. Fear had previously kept her from ever entertaining such a thought, and now it was as if fear itself was pushing her toward independence. She had clearly become afraid of her dependence upon "his majesty," and it dawned upon her that perhaps fear isn't always bad, that maybe sometimes it can even be a friend. But where did this leave her? Despite her awakening need for autonomy, she had no idea where the encampment was... it wasn't as if she could just pack up her things and leave. She stopped walking to ponder this predicament. Looking around at unfamiliar territory, she suddenly realized that she had a more immediate problem to contend with.

She was lost.

· 22 ·

Elliot was attempting to regain his wits with one of his favorite outdoor past-times: archery. It wasn't working. He kept imagining himself skewering the smug reptile; he had to face the fact that Balar had once again gotten under his skin. His anger was only increasing, and he finally put the bow and arrows down and sat on his favorite lawn chair with the tailored cushions. He retrieved a stainless steel flask from the inside pocket of his jacket and drank plentifully. That which he could not control inevitably led him to indulge in spirits. He was too vain and prideful a man to accept his reliance upon the slithering creature, and chose instead to indulge in denial.

Having numbed his consciousness sufficiently, he arose to look for his young protégé. If he couldn't have his way with Balar and the moose, he could at least have it with Lottie. He walked through the compound to her quarters, finding them empty, and searched the enclave, but she was nowhere to be found. Upon inquiry to those he encountered the answers were all the same. No one had seen her. She was not present at the watering hole, and a jaunt out on the ridge top trail where they often walked together was to no avail. There was no Lottie anywhere. His prized trophy appeared to have vanished into the wilderness.

"DRAT!" he exclaimed. "I specifically insisted that she inform me before ever departing the premises!"

Before he could determine how to respond to the predicament, he was confronted by yet another element beyond his control, that being the air space above him. The rumble he'd been hearing had grown in volume, and he looked upward, aghast to see an airplane circling the area. Something in him could sense that this was more than mere coincidence. A film he'd once seen about an assassin journeying up an Asian river suddenly entered his mind. His private domain was no longer as private as he'd assumed. For the first time in his celebrated existence, Elliot Teagartin felt his world beginning to unravel.

Sam and Gil finally looked down upon Elliot and company after being in the air through the later morning and the early afternoon. In accordance with his usual tendency, Sam landed the plane several miles away, presumably a good day's journey from their destination, considering the terrain. He didn't want to take chances with their means of egress, preferring to keep the plane at a safe distance from any possible danger zone. Not knowing what to expect among Teagartin's brood, he didn't want to take chances. Since he first read the dossier, he'd kept in the back of his mind the speculation that the target of the investigation may have ties to the underworld. He was carrying a firearm for protection, and had suggested to Gil that he do the same, but when he sensed how intimidating this was to his traveling companion, he didn't press the point.

The two ate after landing and then set off in mid-afternoon toward their objective. Gil was in a melancholy mood, reflecting upon the years with Nick, and wondering about his own future. He was eager to see Lottie again, though apprehensive about what may have transpired in her life since the last time he'd been with her. Firmly fixed in his memory was that moment a few weeks ago when he looked through Sam's binoculars at Lottie walking down a mountain path with Elliot Teagartin. That recollection led him to question just what his role was in this expedition. Was he rescuing Lottie? Would she even want to be rescued? Whatever the outcome, he was motivated by his love for her, and willing to take the chances necessary to see her again.

The sun was low on the horizon when Sam suddenly turned his head, motioning to Gil to join him behind a large outgrowth of rock on a hillside. He crouched next to Sam, who peered out from behind the sandstone in the direction from which they'd come.

Gil looked at Sam quizzically. "What's up?"

Several seconds passed while Sam focused on the trail behind them before responding. "I think we're being followed." They waited a few more minutes before seeing a lone moose wander toward them up the trail. The creature hesitated before the rock, and Sam cautiously moved from behind their hiding place and faced him. Gil followed. The moose looked intently at them, and then walked past them up the trail before stopping to look back at them again.

Gil spoke first. "Whaddya suppose this is about?"

Sam started down the trail toward the Chosen One. "I don't know for sure, but I get the feeling that we're now supposed to follow him..."

Lottie had been lost in the forest for most of two days, and was feeling weak and dehydrated. At one point she'd come upon a brook with a slow current and drank from it, feeling vaguely sick afterwards. The water hadn't tasted right, and the increasingly frightened state of her thinking had her speculating that an animal may have died in the water upstream. The last time she'd eaten was the night before she set out in the woods.

In an attempt to find her way back to the village, she'd

followed the direction in which the sun was setting, remembering its position back at the encampment, and making assumptions about which way was east, west, north, etc., but could sense that she was only getting more lost as time passed. Nothing looked familiar. She'd come upon no landmark that she recognized from the general area around Elliot's enclave, where she'd often trekked with the Prince and his animals. Regretting the emotional impulsiveness of her behavior, which had brought about this situation, she wondered if she'd benefited at all from Elliot's instruction, and could feel a sense of poor esteem creeping back into her self-awareness. She hardly slept the night before due to rain that had fallen overnight, and was getting sleepy as she trudged onward in her still-damp clothes.

As she sat down to rest on the soft ground in a pine grove, a "buzz" began to cut through the gentle sound of the breeze through the evergreens. It was that creepy telepathic laughter she'd heard often back at the compound. She looked up, and, sure enough, there was Balar looking down at her, his forked tongue slithering in and out. The laughter continued, as the snake seemed amused by the seriousness of Lottie's situation.

"Greetings, wayward child... Can I be of assistance?"

Lottie was too exhausted to respond, and felt herself slowly losing consciousness. Before falling asleep she heard more laughter and a familiar scorn.

"What's the matter, dear? Don't they talk that much down there in Shantytown?"

Calen Foster sat on a cheap motel chair in Sunnyvale listening to the air conditioner hum. It was nine in the morning, and he was in a sour state of mind, having suffered a major bout of insomnia throughout the night. He'd spent a few days driving from the city, and an unfortunate mixture of road weariness and thoughts about his missing friend Artie had conspired to rob him of his sleep. Despite George Cromwell's warnings, he couldn't help it. There was no way to keep this from becoming a vendetta, and he pondered what he would do when he found Teagartin. He imagined holding a gun to the aristocrat bastard's head and watching him cower and plead for his life. Right now, however, he wanted more than anything just to sleep. The stores had been closed the night before by the time he'd settled in and realized his mind wasn't going to stop. The sleepless night had gone on endlessly. "They'd damn well better be open by now!" he thought. He left the room and walked a few blocks to a grocery store, intending to procure an item that had always been a sure fire remedy for his insomnia: red wine. He grabbed a bottle of his preferred brand from the aisle shelf and approached a newspaper rack near the checkout, noticing an article on the front page of a local paper about another Teagartin sighting. He picked up the newspaper, as a cashier looked at him suspiciously.

"...Can I help you with somethin'?"

"Lookin' for someone named Duffy." Cale could detect snickers from the locals within hearing range.

"Whaddya want from that old coot?"

"Never mind... can you just tell me where I can find him?"

"Down at Beechum's Tavern most of the time." More snide laughter ensued.

The sleep-deprived Cale was seriously short on patience, and slammed the bottle of wine down on the counter. "How about telling me where I can find him now?!?..."

The cashier jumped to attention, nervously answering in a stuttering voice. "G-g-g-go out to the other end of town – l-l-last drive on the left... g-goes off the road a ways... y-you'll find his cabin at the end of that d-d-d-drive..."

Cale smiled sardonically. "Thank you, ma'am, that's more like it." He reached for his wallet.

The cashier lifted her hand. "N-n-no, no,...on the house,..."

· 23 ·

They were leaving, one by one, and returning awkwardly to the wild. But not all of them. Some stayed for various reasons. All would agree that they were facing difficult circumstances, but for those in the exodus, life with Elliot had become intolerable. The advantages of Elliot's brand of "civilization" were, for the ones who stayed, simply too hard to relinquish. Perks for some, however, can be curses for others. The food served as a profound case in point. Those with more sturdy constitutions had come to embrace the delectable pleasures in Elliot's recipe file with such aplomb that they just couldn't imagine reverting back to grazing or hunting raw meat. For others with more delicate metabolisms, the continuous indigestion prompted them to throw in the towel and embark upon a transition back to their natural state.

Elliot pretended not to notice, but he could sense that his grip upon the animals was loosening. This did not give him the initiative, however, to change his behavior. In fact, his cantankerous moods seemed to be worsening, and those who remained in his midst resorted to staying out of his way. The sudden absence of Letitia, his beloved student of culture, seemed to spark the change in Elliot that, in turn, caused a considerable percentage of his entourage to depart. Elliot's mood seemed to have evolved overnight from periodic irritability to incessant ill humor. The once affable gentleman was now a continuous curmudgeon who had little, if anything, good to say to anyone. This factor was, for many, the proverbial straw that broke the camel's back. They couldn't stomach such interminable peevishness, and for many with frail digestion, "stomach" was the key word. Elliot's testy countenance only exacerbated the acidity in their sour abdomens. What is often said of man is likewise true for animals: that the way to his heart is through his stomach. In this case, perhaps the reverse would hold validity as well. If the loyalty of an animal was to be compromised, such a process may inevitably involve his or her stomach.

Nearly an hour had passed before Sam detected that the Chosen One was leading them in a different direction than that of Elliot's compound. Or, at least, they had taken a divergent route from the one that he presumed would lead them to the enclave. However, his intuition told him that this was meant to be, that it was somehow part of a greater plan, as unclear as it may seem. He kept quiet with regard to the alternate bearing, not wanting to alarm Gil, whom he knew was eager to reconnect with Lottie. Gil seemed to be none the wiser, and Sam judged it best to keep it that way for now.

As for Gil, he was, at that moment, looking ahead at the Chosen One, and thinking about their previous encounter with the herd of moose dancing to the stereo in the clearing. "Is it odd for a moose to be moving alone through the forest?"

"No, actually," Sam replied. "Moose are generally solitary mammals. What was strange was to see them congregated in a herd like we did, not to mention the stereo and the snake!"

Gil looked at Sam with a puzzled expression. "So, if they usually keep to themselves, what do you suppose was making them come together into a herd?"

"That's the question, and the moose aren't the only ones

to consider... what about the weird behavior from the rest of the animals? It all seems to relate somehow to Teagartin's influence, and I suspect that the snake may have something to do with it also... that serpent was no ordinary reptile. Elliot and the snake may be in cahoots, and who knows who else may be involved?"

Gil thought intently about Sam's response. "So those hokey newspaper articles may have some truth to them?"

Sam nodded. "It sure looks that way, doesn't it?" They hiked quietly for another hour, wondering what they may encounter up ahead. Twilight was approaching as the Chosen One stopped and motioned at them with his head.

Gil was the first to break the silence. "So what's he doing now?"

"Looks like he's trying to point something out to us..." They walked up to the Chosen One. Up ahead lay a pine grove, where Sam thought he detected movement. Sam and Gil approached cautiously until they saw a human form lying prone on the soft ground. Sam was the first to recognize the reclining woman. "Gil... I think it's her..."

Gil ran up to Lottie as fast as his legs could carry him. He sat down on the pine needles next to her, and gently lifted her head into his lap. He felt overjoyed and terrified at the same time, as if the moment of truth was upon him. Lottie's face was scratched and her lips were parched, but he'd never seen anyone look more beautiful. Her eyes slowly opened and she looked up at him, seeing the blurry outline of a man above her. As the man came into focus, tears welled up.

"Gil," she whispered with a dry-throated rasp. "Is it really you?"

"It's me," he replied. With all her strength, she reached her hands upward toward him and smiled. Gil's heart leapt within him.

They pitched a tent in the pine grove and spent the night. Sam let Gil and Lottie have the tent, preferring himself to sleep outside in his sleeping bag on the pine needles and look up at whatever stars may be peering down at him from between the treetops. He felt happy for Gil and Lottie, and could sense that his moment of truth was approaching as well. Before they'd retired for the night, Lottie had regained some strength after getting some food and water in her, and being treated with some of Sam's homeopathic remedies. She'd given account of life in the "Teagartin settlement." Her tales confirmed some of Sam's suspicions, but he hesitated to draw any premature conclusions. This was a journey of personal discovery for Sam, and he needed to see for himself. He didn't feel as if he could trust someone else's perceptions beyond a certain point.

As for the rekindling of Lottie and Gil's relationship, they took up where they last left off, almost as if no time had passed. They spent the night holding onto each other as if they'd sworn a vow to never ever allow themselves to be separated again. The two of them awoke together the next morning to the sound of voices outside the tent. They got up and walked out hand-in-hand into a bright brisk morning to find Sam sitting at a campfire with the Witness. It was a joyful occasion for all as they sat and ate together and discussed recent events. Gil felt particularly awestruck, having not had the opportunity previously to interact with the Witness. The Chosen One suddenly appeared from out of a thicket at one juncture of the conversation.

"I see that my messenger found you." The Witness seemed to be referring to the Chosen One, and both Sam and Gil felt that this explained the mystery of how the moose had appeared and led them to Lottie.

Gil, however, was interested in other overarching mysteries. "Please forgive me for asking, but who, exactly, are you? And who, exactly, is Elliot Teagartin?"

The Witness smiled at him lovingly. "You are indeed a man who comes to the point. It would be premature right now for me to tell you who I am. I think you'll know in time. For now, just think of me as a 'guardian.' As for who Mr. Teagartin is, that's what the four of you are here to find out, and I hope you'll take heart in knowing that I'll be with you every step of the way. There's a rock quarry pond about a half-mile west of the village. You can find it by heading down the ridge top trail until it leads downhill to the quarry. Mr. Teagartin goes there often in the late afternoon before the evening meal. He'll often take a swim in the pond if he's sure no one is watching. It will be there that you'll see him..."

At this, the Witness arose to greet the Chosen One. Sam got up and doused the fire, while Gil and Lottie collapsed the tent. As they prepared to leave, they looked down a trail toward the "village" to see the Witness departing with the Chosen One. He turned around and waved at them before the two disappeared over the horizon. Sam smiled and breathed in the clean morning air. "You see that? Now there's a real St. Francis..."

Another sunny day descended on Sunnyvale. Cale was caught up on his sleep, having slept through most of the day and even through a good part of the following night. Mid-morning had arrived after his sleep-fest, and he was turning into Duffy's pockmarked driveway, per the grocery cashier's directions. He drove slowly down a straight-a-way through scrub forest, and around a few bends until he came upon a dilapidated log home with a small barn and a large pen off to the side containing horses. He parked off to the side of the drive a ways from the cabin, and approached on foot to take in the surroundings. He noticed a moped parked in front next to a well pump, and an outhouse down a path to the left. Several strong raps on the front door failed to produce a response. Lifting the latch, he detected that the door was unlocked, and slowly opened it.

"Anybody home?" He took the liberty of entering, seeing a rough one-room interior with a loft. As he looked around the dwelling for signs of life, it appeared that no one was in the loft. Then, he spotted the end of a bed with two calloused feet extending out from under a blanket in a room off to the right. He rounded the corner to see an old bearded codger lying face up, asleep on a ratty twin bed under an old woolen blanket that looked half-chewed up by mice or eaten by moths. Empty liquor bottles littered what little "furniture" there was. The man on the bed looked like a homeless decrepit Santa Claus sleeping on a flophouse cot.

"Mr. Duffy? Mr. Duffy?" The man snorted suddenly and sat up on the bed. Pushing himself up onto his feet, he walked past Cale and across the main part of the room to a closet, opening the door and reaching in. Cale suddenly found himself staring down the double barrel of a shotgun, and dived to the floor. The gun went off with a thunderous boom, spraying buckshot in Cale's general direction.

"Who the hell are you, and what're you doing here?!"

Cale scrambled to get under the bed, finding himself face-to-face with a gently growling Doberman Pincer.

"I repeat... who are you and what the hell are you doin' in my house?!"

"Can you call off your dog?"

"ROSCOE, GET OVER HERE!" The dog obeyed. "MISTER, YOU'VE GOT FIVE SECONDS TO ANSWER MY QUESTIONS BEFORE I FIRE OFF ANOTHER ROUND!"

"I'm from the city..."

"Well now... you just increased your chances of gittin' shot"

"...I'm a friend of Sam Crowfeather!"

There was a break in the tension.

"Come out from under there and lemme get a look at

you..." Cale crawled out and stood up, facing Duffy, the shotgun, and Roscoe, who was drooling out of one side of his mouth as he bared his teeth and continued growling.

"My name's Calen Foster. I'm a reporter with the Tribune."

"Well, you've answered one part of the question... gimme the other half, and I may just put down this double-ought."

"I need a guide into the forest... Sam recommended you..."

Duffy pointed to one of the chairs at the table. "Sit down over there..."

Cale slowly eased past Roscoe and sat down. The dog's eyes were glued to his every movement.

"ROSCOE, GO LAY DOWN... you're bein' rude to our guest..." Again he complied, resuming his spot under the bed. Duffy sat down on the chair opposite Cale and put the gun on the table.

"Look, I know I'm trespassing and all, but would you mind pointing that in another direction?"

Duffy shook his head from side-to-side, stood up, and leaned the gun against the cabin wall before sitting back down. "You've got a lot of nerve, you know that? You're damn lucky I'm not diggin' your grave right now. You wouldn't be the first..."

Cale swallowed hard, suspecting he'd made a mistake approaching this guy. Before he had a chance to say anything, Duffy spoke again.

"A hundred dollars a day, in advance..."

Cale pointed in the direction of the pen. "Can we use your horses over there?" Duffy grabbed a half-empty gin bottle and took a slug.

"...I s'pose so. So what are we lookin' for?"

Cale swallowed again. He might as well just come out with it. "Elliot Teagartin..."

Duffy looked down at the table and shook his head again. "Shit! I figured as much..."

"Sam indicated that it was about 10 miles northwest, where two streams-"

"Don't bother with the directions... I know where it is, or at least I know where it was 'bout three weeks ago... gimme the rest of the day t' get ready. We can leave tomorrow mornin', around 9 am... you'd best bring that money with you tomorrow. Count on around 5 days there and back..." Cale arose silently, departed the cabin, and drove back to the motel, still feeling the sting of some of the buckshot on his legs. He seriously wondered if he would be returning from the upcoming excursion alive.

· 24 ·

Father Dominic was feeling hopeful for the first time in quite a while. He'd briefed his superiors on Sam's findings, and hadn't heard from them since. This was unusual. He'd been barraged with calls from Father Joe and others on a daily basis until the briefing. These were generally casual calls, disguised as serious inquiries. These men seemed to have little else to do but imagine that problems existed where there weren't any, and when there were real issues, they were generally mole hills that his superiors insisted upon turning into mountains. And then there were the crises that they'd become adept at covering up and ignoring. Too many times he'd been assigned to arrange for a priest's departure to another diocese after serious charges of child molestation had been brought forth.

Since the briefing, however, he hadn't been contacted once, which he mistakenly mistook as a positive development. He sat outside on his back patio table eating Italian food and enjoying a glass of Chianti. He delighted in the various winged creatures that landed on, and ate from, his bird feeders, and greatly enjoyed their songs. Then, there was an intrusion. It was the telephone. Should he ignore it? He let it ring a few more times and then made the ill-fated decision to answer. "Hello?..."

"Fr. Dominic, this is Fr. Joe. Turn on your TV., Channel 13. I think we've hit the jackpot this time! Call me later and let me know what you think..."

Fr. Dominic hung up the phone, noticing from the wall clock that it was straight up 8 o'clock. Prime time. He picked up the remote and clicked on the tube. The first thing he heard was a drumroll and a lot of audience hoopla. The camera panned from a Hollywood sound stage to a restless audience and back. Then an announcer broke into the chatter and the audience quieted down, no doubt signaled by a teleprompter.

"...And now, ladies and gentlemen, it's time to play 'ORIGINAL SIN!' with your host, who's the most with the Holy Ghost, FATHER VIC QUIZMO!"

The host came out from behind a curtain onto the stage. "...Domini, Domini, Domini, Domini... Welcome to the show, folks, good to have you with us. We've got a date with destiny for YOU on ORIGINAL SIN!"

The audience erupted into cheers and applause, and drumrolls resumed.

"...And now, it's time to introduce our hostess, your favorite devil's advocate, and certainly mine, Miss BAMBI BOMBOZA!"

Bambi wiggled herself suggestively onto the stage, and blew a kiss to the audience.

"Does that girl have talent, or what?" The audience continued to applaud and cheer wildly.

"...But, seriously, folks, let's not tarry any longer in meeting today's contestants. Bambi, tell us a little about them!"

The spotlight focused upon the voluptuous Ms. Bomboza. "Oooooh, Fr. Vic, here they are from Des Moines, Nebraska – he's a Sanitation Engineer for a major chemical corporation... she's a Librarian and part-time mother, meet JIM AND MIMI VAN CLEVE!" The contestants entered and kissed Fr. Vic's over-sized mood ring.

Fr. Dominic hit the off button on the remote and fell down into a sitting position on the couch. He was speechless. He sat for a few minutes, finding it difficult to collect his thoughts.

"How could they!" he repeated several times to himself. "They've lost any sense of shame!" His blood began to boil as he considered how the situation had degenerated fully into dollars and cents, into pandering to the lowest common denominator. This was it, he told himself. This was his moment of truth. If he had any sense of decency, this was the time to call it quits.

About an hour down the trail they caught up with the Chosen One. The Witness had apparently departed once again for the invisible realm. The four of them moved along at a leisurely pace, not being in a hurry. They'd get there soon enough, and the overall mood combined eagerness with cautious apprehension. For a period of time Sam held up the rear, walking alone with his thoughts. Looking ahead of him at Lottie, Gil, and the Chosen One, he couldn't help but remember scenes out of the Wizard of Oz. The four of them made quite a team, and Sam marveled over the prospect of such a journey with three disparate individuals, all of whom he'd known for less than a month. Already they felt like lifelong friends, and a sense of mysterious providence seemed to bind them together.

They began to notice an interesting phenomenon as they moved forward. Various mammals were traveling toward them through the forest; the animals acknowledged their presence in a telling manner, as if they were departing from the very destination toward which Sam and his friends were headed. Lottie recognized some of them from her time at the village, and said hello as they passed by. An hour up the trail, Sam looked ahead to see that the three had stopped to rest and eat at what could be described as a scenic overlook – a high point where they could see for miles. The picturesque vista was comprised of a vast plain interspersed with forest.

As Sam approached, Gil looked in his direction. "Could I borrow your binoculars for a minute?"

Sam retrieved the instrument from his pack and handed it to Gil, while Lottie sat eating from a package of trail mix.

Gil slowly cased the area before them. "Wow... there's more and more of them... the ones we saw back there seemed kinda confused..."

He handed the binoculars back to Sam, who proceeded to take a look himself.

"Yeah, there are a lot of them... more than you'd expect to see, and the predators don't appear to have reverted back to their old ways, not yet at any rate...."

Lottie put down the trail mix and reached for some bottled water. "So whaddya think's goin' on up there where we're headed?"

Sam continued to survey the wayward animals in the wilderness before them. "I don't know for sure, but to risk a cliché, I suspect there must be trouble in paradise!"

There was one more sip in the flask. It wouldn't be enough. Not nearly enough. His appetite for drink had grown considerably. Morning still dragged on and he was drinking already. A frenetic check in the kitchen and another in the storage area both yielded negative results. Elliot had never known failure until recently. In his quiet preoccupation with his worsening circumstances, he could now add another failure to the list. He was a failed alcoholic. He'd taken his eyes off the ball, and now there was one sip in the flask that stood between him and the utter desolation that would surely ensue from the depletion of the liquor supply. He had no recourse but to replenish his supply of Glenlivet by means of a quick trip back to the realm of men, a world he hadn't inhabited since before he parachuted out of his airplane.

"Let's see..." he thought, "...there is a town somewhere to

the southeast..." He fetched the map that he kept with the literature next to the recliner.

"Ah yes, 'Sunnyvale'... sounds like a retirement home." He contemplated the possibilities. He'd saddle the horses, and could be there in time to get back before dark. He'd bring some heavy-duty rucksacks, and... "Oh... I'll need a disguise of some sort...." He rooted around in the storage area where the animals kept a "novelty bin" and a collection of obscure clothing. There he found some sunglasses, overalls, and work boots. "That should do the trick." He saddled the horses and donned the disguise, and, "Oh, I almost forgot an essential element!" Looking positively ridiculous, Elliot walked through the compound to his sleeping quarters. The remaining animals stared at him slack-jawed as if they were witnessing an unimaginable psychiatric disintegration. He found the footlocker under his hammock, pulled it out and opened it, and.... "No! NO! IT SIMPLY CANNOT BE!" But it was. He emptied the contents onto the Persian rug next to the hammock, only to find his fear confirmed.

His wallet was missing.

· 25 ·

Indeed trouble was brewing in paradise. As the four intrepid explorers approached the settlement, what was once a dynamic thriving community populated by eager apostles, appeared now through the binoculars to be empty. But not quite. They could detect some movement, if they focused long enough on a given area. Delectable odors that seemed to originate from something gourmet wafted through the travelers' senses.. Whatever the origin, it didn't smell like typical campfire food.

"Boy, I'm hungry!" Gil commented. "Trail mix sure doesn't seem appetizing after smelling that. Whaddya suppose it is?"

Sam put down the binoculars. "I don't know, but if we want to interface with Teagartin by late afternoon, we'd better find that quarry." They weren't sure where the ridge top trail was in reference to where they were, but assumed they'd find it if they circled around to the south. As it turned out, they were closer than they thought. Twenty minutes later they found the path, and the four proceeded toward the quarry, coming to a fork in the path. One trail led to the left steeply downhill, and the other to the right curved and then turned parallel, heading down a more gradual slope.

"So which do we take?" Gil inquired.

Sam thought for a moment. "My gut tells me that we should wait for him in hiding. I know it's rather arbitrary, but I'd rather be looking down at him than looking up, so I say let's take the one with the more gentle slope." Sam started to the right and the rest of them followed. They reached an area that was increasingly rocky the further they walked, until they were walking on quarry-sized blocks of rock. Then, the rock abruptly ended at a cliff. Thirty feet down the cliff lay the quarry pond with a small shore of rough pebbles. Sam looked down to the left, spotting a path to the shore.

"This is perfect, that is, if he takes the fork that leads to the water down there. We'll hide up here and wait for him."

Lottie felt herself becoming fearful. "But what if he takes the path we took and comes up behind us?"

Sam was at a loss for a good answer. "We'll just have to take that chance... anyway, he'll be sorely outnumbered, so either way we'll be okay." Sam had been less than honest in his attempt to reassure Lottie. He was actually getting nervous. Some kind of a dark presence clung to these woods and he knew that the normal rules of engagement didn't apply in occult situations. Just because there were four of them and only one adversary didn't necessarily mean that they were safe.

Just then, however, he felt the invisible presence of a hand on his shoulder. A faint voice whispered in his ear. "It's okay. Just stay where you are."

No more than five minutes passed before they saw a figure emerging from the woods. It was Elliot Teagartin, dressed in swimming attire, carrying a towel. He appeared somewhat dazed and a little depressed - a subtle contrast to the public image he'd projected for so long. He walked onto the shore, looking apprehensively around him as if he suspected that someone may be watching. On the top of the cliff the four kept hidden to the best of their ability as they looked down upon him.

A sudden fit of hay fever had its way with Lottie and she

sneezed. The four of them moved their heads back from the cliff's edge. Elliot looked around him. He knew that voice. "It seems that my betrayer may be at hand," he mumbled to himself. He turned back around and pondered whether he should take a swim. Several tense moments passed, and the four slowly eased their heads forward where they could see him once again.

They observed as Elliot leaned forward and gazed into the pond, at which point the water transformed his reflection into the most hideous, repugnant spectacle. The macabre vision jumped upward out of the water toward them, invading their bodies through their eyes, causing their limbs to convulse, their skin to burn, and their stomachs to roll in fits of nausea. The face of incomprehensible depravity consumed them whole as if they were watching a 3D horror movie that projected and transformed its hellish blood-fest into their own gruesome circumstance. They gasped for air, feeling as if the breath had been sucked out of them, and turned their heads away, covering their eyes with their hands, but to no avail. They found the monstrous mirror image melded to their sight as well as their other senses. An overwhelmingly putrid sulfuric stench engulfed the entire area.

Elliot then stood up straight as if he'd seen nothing but his own tedious reflection in the water. Suspecting that he was being watched, he removed his sandal and dipped his foot into the water before turning to leave.

"Come on in, the water's fine!"

He'd come back. The Chosen One had returned to the fold. His preaching resumed, but this time it struck somewhat of a chord with his brothers and sisters. At first, his reports of the ghastly vision of Elliot and his abandonment by his followers seemed to them like idle tales, but there came a point when they actually turned off the ghetto blaster and listened to him. They'd noticed several bewildered animals passing through their area over the past few days from the direction of Teagartin's enclave, and this seemed to lend credence to the Chosen One's reports. They kept this information in the back of their minds as one of them reached down to turn the boombox back on.

Meanwhile, Balar was hatching a plan. The moose were running dangerously low on batteries for the stereo, and none of them desired to raid Elliot's encampment after hearing the Chosen One's eerie tales.

In the clearing the moose gathered around the two remaining batteries, and urged the Chosen One to do his duty and insert them into the back of the stereo, which was already showing signs of running out of power.

The Chosen One reluctantly agreed, but used this as a ministerial opportunity to appeal to the moose, standing resolutely before them and looking into their impatient eyes. "Before I insert these last two batteries, you must listen to me. There will come a time in which there will be no batteries left. What will you do then? You will most certainly taste of the bitter consequences of your idolatry. You have a golden opportunity before you now, to wean yourself off of this monstrous device and return to the natural state you enjoyed before this influence bludgeoned its way into your lives. You must return before it's too late!"

Balar looked down from a poplar branch, swinging subtly toward them and interjecting with an elevated buzz, gaining their attention in a vaguely hypnotic manner. "He says you should return. Return to what? Wandering around aimlessly, each of you by yourself? Grazing for your food? Where would your music come from? The birds? The wind? The rain? Could you withstand such loneliness and boredom? I think not... I think not."

The Chosen One continued. "You were happy before all this happened... don't you remember? There was no anger, bitterness, or contention among you! There was a primordial balance between your solitary contemplative existence, and the periodic necessity of coming together as a herd. You bore your children and raised them properly. They respected you then, do they now? For the sake of your precious children and of future generations, I beg of you, take steps to return to your natural state! You must return!"

The herd repetitively looked back and forth from the Chosen One to Balar as if they were watching a tennis match in slow motion at Wimbledon. Finally, Balar threw a leather object down at the herd and returned the winning volley.

"I know where you can get all the batteries you need..."

· 26 ·

It was as if time had been suspended back at that quarry pond. They had no idea how many hours they'd laid at the top of that cliff, but when they finally arose, the Chosen One was nowhere to be found. When passing by the village, they caught another glimpse of Elliot through the binoculars. He was dressed formally and seated in a slumped position. Aside from horses, they could see no other animals in his midst, and they wondered if the remnants had now dispersed. For reasons unclear even to him, Sam couldn't resist confronting Elliot, though he was unsure as to what, exactly, a face-to-face encounter would accomplish. He asked his friends to stay put where they were and wait for him, and he set off in the direction of the encampment.

Meanwhile, Elliot sat in his easy chair brooding over his distant past, vaguely attempting to explain to his own satisfaction why his situation had so rapidly deteriorated. He was trying, in vain, to find someone or something to blame for his predicament. He could easily blame Balar, but deep down Elliot knew that the snake could hardly be held accountable for everything. Perhaps, if he was honest with himself, Elliot could blame the snake for a lot less that he had previously thought. He felt at that moment like an orphan, but was at a loss to comprehend the sensation of loneliness that engulfed his awareness. For this he blamed Lottie and the animal disciples who'd abandoned him. And then there were his parents. Ah, yes... Reginald and Margaret. He could always blame them for his shortcomings, assuming that he might have any personal faults that could have contributed to the current state of his affairs. Elliot's psychological make-up led him to relate in a different manner to his two parents when they were alive. He had never understood his mother Margaret, and had come to see her ardent Catholicism and devotion to St. Francis of Assisi, as well as her pious attitudes and behaviors, as merely unfortunate weaknesses to which those of the "gentler sex" were prone. As such he generally ignored Margaret, treating her as if she was invisible. As for his father, however, Elliot was indeed "a chip off the old block," though his father, Reginald, knew early on that his son's breadth of intellect and talent far surpassed his own. Reginald played along with his wife's religious sensibilities, but would often react, during her rambling discourses on the faith, with "a wink and a nod" in Elliot's direction. Reginald, like his son, had an interest in the supernatural, motivated by a need for otherworldly experiences that satisfied his curiosity more immediately than those achieved through the gradual awakenings of the Church. Such esoteric leanings made Reginald a rather unusual aristocrat for his time, and Elliot looked to his father for guidance on channeling his gifts and talents.

Elliot was, however, disappointed by Reginald's counsel, that is, until his father provided him with some formative adventures that would afford him the direction he craved. The pilgrimages taken by Reginald and Elliot to remote jungles in Central America provided a missing piece to the labyrinthine puzzle that came to be Elliot Teagartin. These trips, during which Elliot studied extensively under shamans and medicine men, fulfilled his need for mystical acumen. The ways these two men were affected by these experiences sharply differed, however. The content of this instruction disturbed Reginald, whereas Elliot, having become increasingly fascinated as he went along, continued to indulge in trips to these remote regions long after his father had ceased to do so. In time, he became adept at the techniques taught by the shamans, which, when combined with his considerable talent in the use of hypnotism acquired through previous studies in the field of Psychology, amassed considerable power to the tenuous psyche of Francis Elliot Teagartin. And, finally, it was during one of these periods of study in Central America, that Elliot first met and allied himself with the reptile Balar.

Presently, however, Elliot felt anything but powerful as he sat alternately staring down at the ground, and then up at a corral of horses nearby, the only animals that remained in his enclave. His empire in the Northern Wilderness had crumbled; he knew that something had to be done. As he sat contemplating the past, he heard a rustling in some brush, and out stepped Sam Crowfeather, who approached until he stood facing Elliot at a midway point between him and his horses. The depressed magnate seemed hardly surprised by the intrusion, and half-heartedly began a conversation, barely looking up at Sam. "Hello stranger... enjoy your dip in the pool? I'd offer you a drink, but I'm afraid the supply is depleted."

Sam said nothing in response.

Noticing Sam's hand resting upon what appeared to be a concealed firearm, Elliot continued. "Are you an assassin, by chance?"

"No."

"A curiosity-seeker? Where's your camera?"

"I suppose you could say I'm curious, but I don't have a camera."

"Well, I'm afraid your timing is rather unfortunate... you're likely to be disappointed."

Again, Sam said nothing.

Sam's reluctance to speak was beginning to make Elliot nervous. It was then that the memory of the plane circling the enclave a few days back popped into his head. "Just who are you anyway? What are your intentions, if I might ask?"

Sam continued his silence.

"Well? Out with it! Here's your once-in-a-lifetime chance, an exclusive interview with the celebrity of the century! What the hell are you waiting for?"

Continued silence. A tense minute passed as the two men stared at each other, before Elliot made a final plea with a puzzled expression. "Who are you?"

"Oh... I guess you could say I'm a voice crying out in the wilderness."

The circumstances of the moment were such that Sam's assertion was welcome relief to the beleaguered aristocrat. Elliot found the reply hilarious, and began laughing uproariously for the first time in months, before regaining his composure. "WELL, GOOD LUCK!" Elliot exclaimed, slapping his knees and succumbing to further howling laughter.

The man sitting before him appeared pitiful to Sam, despite the momentary levity. He saw no point in continuing the conversation, and turned away to disappear into the forest. Sam could hear Elliot's highly animated mirth resound and echo through the trees for a considerable period of time.

Sam, Gil, and Lottie trudged through the wilderness back to the plane. They hadn't eaten for the past few days, feeling too sick for food. It was a struggle to keep from getting dehydrated. They threw up most of the water they'd consumed, and had hardly slept since leaving for the plane. They now faced a profound depth of exhaustion.

It was just as well for Sam that he hadn't eaten or slept, for this had given him the opportunity to continuously revel in thought. He'd found what he was looking for, having peeked into the soul of a great Western man, who'd achieved a level of affluence, fame, and power, of which many mortals wouldn't dare dream. It grieved him to think that this is what countless others aspired to achieve at any cost. If they only knew. He could have been seduced in such a direction, and at that moment, despite his weariness and depletion, he considered himself the most fortunate man alive. He could see what the Elliot Teagartins, J.P. Morgans, Rockefellers and Rothchilds of this world risked spiritually to attain such levels of greatness; he had finally reached the point that he wanted no part of it. The Red Man in him had won the battle for his soul. He knew that he was a deeply flawed man, but with the help of the Great Spirit, the God-Man who was nailed to the tree, his ancestors, and all of the saints who had ever walked the face of this earth, he could triumph over the Teagartin in his own soul, and walk into the light of eternal blessedness.

Sam had, at last, found his true identity. Deep down, however, he knew that this process of discovery was not an end in itself. His mother's words from weeks ago came back to him: "When we sacrifice our wants and desires and focus on the needs of others, we find our identity." In addition to the example provided by his mother, Sam had found someone who could teach him to use his gifts to benefit his fellow man, a more potent role model – The Witness.

· 27 ·

It was a lovely day at the Sunnyvale Walmart. Mrs. Velma Merkel stood in the entrance with her cane, proud to embark upon another exciting shift in her capacity as a Greeter. She loved her job. Despite some of the colorful characters she encountered at the Super-Center, her job rarely surprised her, which she preferred, considering her nerves and her generally declining health. She was a widow living on a fixed income, and to work as a Greeter fit her needs and life situation like a glove. She said a hearty "Hello!" and "Welcome to Walmart!" to all the folks who came in from the stretches of the Northern Wilderness. Velma was eager to be of assistance in serving the needs of these customers.

Suddenly, however, she detected a commotion occurring outside in the parking lot. She could hear the sound of screeching brakes, squealing tires, auto collisions and yelling, screaming voices. It sounded like pandemonium out there! She bravely stood her ground, per the requirements in her job description, and nervously wondered what she was about to experience. And then, there they were, a large herd of moose heading right for the entrance! They were too impatient for the automatic doors and just crashed right through.

"Oh my!" Heavy-duty glass was spraying in all directions.

Velma shook in fear as the herd approached her. "Heavens to Betsy... why they're even bigger than they look in the picture books I've seen..."

The moose stopped in front of her, too close for comfort.

"Uhh... welcome to Wal-Mart!"

The moose in the front had a compact stereo in his mouth, and another pointed his antlers repeatedly at an empty compartment on the back.

"Uhh... batteries? Why, that would be in aisle 22..."

The herd moved past her on either side. The cashiers and people in the checkout screamed and scattered in every direction as the moose crashed their way through, knocking over several of the cash registers. Coins bounced off the floor in numerous directions, while bills fluttered through the air like confetti. Several of the moose pushed shopping carts with their antlers, some of which fell over crashing to the floor. Someone in the store pulled the fire alarms. The moose were too big for the aisles. Merchandise, merchandise racks, and special product displays flew in every direction as the moose approached aisle 22. They filled the shopping carts with all the batteries they could find and turned around, trampling the strewn products on the floor as they approached checkout.

The moose hung doubled shopping bags stuffed with batteries on their antlers and headed for the decimated doorway. The police, fire department, and animal control arrived, but stood by helplessly as the large animals exited. The last moose through the checkout threw down the leather object that Balar had given them. It landed in an open position next to the only cash register left standing. A terrified cashier looked down on an open wallet full of cash and charge cards. Displayed prominently was Elliot Teagartin's driver's license.

As the last moose exited, Velma continued to stand her ground. "Have a nice day... y'all come back!"

Father Dominic put the last boxed-up collection of his belongings in the trunk of his Mercedes. These were among the few things that he was keeping. All of his furniture and appliances, and most of the other items in his house had been put up for auction, with the stipulation that the proceeds be given to a local charity that provided food and housing assistance for the poor and destitute. All he was keeping were some clothes, toiletries, and a few other odds and ends and keepsakes... things that would fit in the back seat or trunk of his car.

He walked past the "For Sale" sign in his front lawn and back into the empty house, trying to remember what the last thing was that he had to do before leaving. Yesterday morning, he'd closed all of his bank accounts and put his house up for sale. The realtor hadn't wasted any time – the sign was on his lawn by late that afternoon. He'd also gotten rid of his phones and cancelled his phone numbers to ensure there would be no further contact between him and his superiors, while purchasing a mobile phone to which he'd given the new number to no one except the realtor. He would be mailing a package to Father Joe on his way out, which contained his clerical shirt and collar. The package would have no note or return address. They would surely make the connection sooner or later, after wondering why his phones had been disconnected, and why he was nowhere to be found. They could interpret all of this however they wished. For the first time in many years, Fr. Dominic felt as if he was being true to his original calling, and felt strongly that God was nudging him in the direction he was now taking. He no longer cared what his superiors might think of his actions.

Standing in the kitchen, he attempted to engage his memory. "Now what was I going to do? Oh yes... the letter to Sam!" He sat on the floor with a piece of paper and a pen, writing the letter against the linoleum.

Sam,

I'm finally doing what I should have done years ago. No more involving myself in the tawdry affairs of a sinking ship. I'm heading out west. The Church is alive and survives somewhere, and I'm off to find it. As wretched as I am, I'll nonetheless take my place among the remaining believers, wherever they are. God willing, I'll even become a solitary desert-dweller if I have to.

Hope to see you again some day in this world or the next. May God's abundant blessings be upon you, Sam.

Your friend,
Fr. Dominic

The Priest folded the letter and put it in an envelope, writing Sam's address and affixing postage. He put the letter and the package to Fr. Joe on the passenger seat in the front of the car, and turned the ignition. Dropping the letter and package into a drive-up mailbox at the post office, he pulled out and onto the city street, heading for the freeway. The sun was setting in the west as he drove up the interstate ramp. He put the Mercedes in high gear and sped west into the scarlet horizon to begin a new life.

They hadn't been on the trail an hour before Cale smelled something familiar. Duffy rode up front and pulled a pack horse behind him, while Cale held up the rear. Marijuana smoke wafted from the front horse to the back, and floods of associated memories washed over Cale. He was reminded in particular of his college days when he'd first encountered Arthur Dinsmore. He and some of his friends would, on occasion, get high before attending a lecture from the controversial figure.

Professor Dinsmore would never be granted tenure, in part due to his radical counter-culture perspective, but mostly as a result of his refusal to cotton to an academic culture that placed an inordinate emphasis upon research, and continues to do so. Artie loved only to teach, and, as such, he knew that his days in academia would be numbered. He loathed academic research, which wasn't to say that he disliked writing. He loved to write cutting edge human-interest stories, and accepted the necessity of going to work in the "real world" without the slightest hesitation. From that point onward, Artie would drive editors under who worked to drink with his eccentric unorthodox methods of journalism, yet gain the begrudging respect of a good many of his colleagues at large.

Cale appreciated the trip down memory lane, but was simultaneously concerned about the functional capacity of his kooky guide and tracker. Duffy was already three sheets to the wind when Cale had first encountered him that morning, and now he was adding pot to the mix, and a rather potent strain at that. Cale felt himself getting a significant contact high just from the second hand smoke. He'd felt more than a little uncomfortable that morning handing $500 to a disheveled drunk who looked as if he'd slept on a park bench. The young reporter was especially alarmed at one point when they rounded a bend on the trail and Duffy dismounted. There, in a clearing before them, stood a healthy looking crop of homegrown ganja, undoubtedly Duffy's personal "garden." Cale looked down at him pointedly.

"Need I remind you of why we embarked on this journey?" Duffy reached into one of the bags on the pack horse.

"Shut up and give me a hand." He threw a sheathed machete in Cale's direction, noting his look of disapproval. "Look, if you want to continue on your own, that's fine with me. It ain't too late to get a partial refund..."

Cale caught the machete and sighed. He really didn't want

to go it alone, recalling the previous trip when he'd gone around in circles before coming upon Sam. A capable guide was necessary, and he decided to trust that Sam knew what he was doing when he recommended this guy. The two spent ten minutes harvesting weed before sitting down for a bite to eat.

For the sake of satisfying his curiosity, Cale struck up a conversation. "So... I hear you used to hang around with the Beat Poets?"

Duffy swallowed the last bite of a sandwich and swigged on some gin before firing up another joint. "That was a long time ago... 25 years? It was just a brief passing phase. I met some of them through a friend I had at the time who would bring me along. She had some sort of dalliance goin' with Corso... evidently she thought I'd fit right in, but I was no writer. Never met Keroac... only met Burroughs once, but he didn't leave much of an impression on me... Cassady was a wild child! Wasn't fond of Ferlinghetti – something squirrelly 'bout him. Ginsberg seemed like a kid who never grew up, always frolicking in a city park somewhere. My favorite of the bunch was Gary Snyder – had a rural sensibility like mine, but honestly, I didn't know any of 'em very well, and I wasn't around 'em all that often. I was only in the city a few years – didn't like it. I'm really a small town guy at heart..." He offered the joint to Cale, who declined. "It's interesting that you'd bring up the Beat Poets, though, considering who we're lookin' for right now."

Cale was suddenly intrigued. "What do you mean?"

Duffy ingested another swallow of gin. "Well... I may appear to be some old idiot geezer washed up in booze, but I am a historian of sorts, and I've done a lot of reading in modern philosophy. There's an interesting relationship between Teagartin and the Beatniks."

Cale was surprised indeed at the level of cognitive activity coming his way from Duffy, and was interested in the particulars of his commentary. "Go on..."

"You see, in the post-World War II era when I came of age, you had this rapid evolution of consumer culture that was wrapped up in notions of 'The American Dream.' Elliot Teagartin's idea of 'Virtuous Consumerism' added a philosophical framework to this development. The voice of the so-called 'beat generation' was the first notable sign of popular vocal dissent in response. The writings of the Beat Poets questioned, and essentially condemned, this prevailing notion of the 'American Dream.' To them, Teagartin's philosophy was phony, vapid, and spiritually bankrupt, and they wanted no part of it..." Cale sat looking at his guide and marveled at how appearances can be deceiving.

Duffy stood up and stretched his back. "Well... we're not gettin' any closer to him by sittin' here talkin'..." He wrapped the harvested marijuana in plastic and tied it to the packhorse. They resumed their journey down the trail. Though he didn't say anything to Cale about it, Duffy noticed several times that there were horse tracks leading in the opposite direction back to Sunnyvale. Cale began to focus his thoughts on getting closer to Elliot Teagartin with each passing moment.

Unbeknownst to these two men, they were being watched. Balar looked down upon them from a shagbark hickory. He had just disposed of a fly in the ointment. Having sealed the fate of the lone dissenting voice, there was now nothing standing in his way. He was on the verge of breaking into "The Big Time" with his moose troupe, and was delighted in the determination and perseverance he sensed in the newspaper reporter on horseback below him. The young man would eventually catch up with Elliot, and that suited Balar just fine. Elliot no longer served his purposes, and might as well self-destruct. "Ah, yes... Mr. Foster... keep your eyes on the prize... despite the setbacks, you will eventually triumph and indulge your sense of justice. Go forth now, you have my blessing..."

Sam, Gil, and Lottie suddenly found themselves together in the forest. Sam looked at Gil and Lottie, and they looked back at Sam. All three of them were confused. They'd spent a considerable amount of time together in the Northern Wilderness. There was only one problem. All three of them had been back in the so-called "civilized world" of humankind for the past few days. When they were last in these woods, they'd made it back to the plane, where they spent the night, and flew back to the city the next day. Gil and Lottie dropped Sam off at his flat, and then took the jeep out to the little town where Lottie and her father had previously resided.

So what were they doing back in the forest? How did they get there? A bright light over the next hill seemed to be beckoning them. They walked over the crest of the hill to see the Witness waving at them near the foot of a cliff that looked to be 100 feet high. He was standing next to a mound of earth covered with flowers and appeared to be praying quietly. They were glad to see him and approached, somehow knowing that he'd called them all together again.

The Witness smiled at them and spoke. "I'm happy to see you again, although the occasion might not be as joyous as we would choose. Our dear brother the moose is buried here. I thought it important for you to know. He returned to the herd, where he stood alone until the end. Despite all of his efforts, they would not listen. They would not turn back, and instead became hostile, cornering him on that cliff up there and pushing him off. Our comrade truly fought the good fight. All I would ask is that you reserve a spot for him in your hearts, that you keep alive the memory of this great warrior spirit, who sacrificed himself for others. There is no greater love than that."

The four solemnly stood there together at the burial mound mourning their fallen friend. The light that drew the three of them to the Witness intensified until they felt themselves enveloped in its brightness. They felt a rush of energy come over them and they were lighter than air, carried back to a moment nearly a week ago, when they were breaking camp to head toward the village. In the distance they saw the Witness walking down the trail with the Chosen One. The Witness turned around to wave at them, and the Chosen One turned and looked at the three of them one last time before they turned back around and walked over the horizon into the light. Sam, Gil, and Lottie awoke the next morning in the domain of men, with this memory fresh in their minds.

· 28 ·

The two lovebirds had hit upon an idea. Lottie and Gil had been back at the Crump's mobile home for a few weeks, and had just gotten married a few days before in a hastily arranged ceremony at a local Baptist Church, where Lottie and Daddy were once members. The occasion had given both of them an opportunity to reconnect with their extended families, and on the day of the ceremony, the Church entertained an odd mixture of Gil's French relatives and Lottie's Appalachian kin. Sam Crowfeather was also present.

They were embarking upon another labor of love, a genuine reflection of their empathy for, and desire to provide assistance to, those less fortunate. They were taking steps to form a charitable foundation with the leftover fortune from the Lotto winnings, which was still a considerable sum, even after taxes, and what Daddy'd squandered. The two of them were to be executors of the foundation, and to assist them as manager of the estate, they'd hired John Guhrman, who was only too happy to forsake his pathetic government salary for this far more lucrative opportunity. The details were still being worked out, but they weren't in a hurry. They felt as if they could take their time.

Beyond all of that, the two of them were just enjoying each

other's company, and doing some traveling. Sam Crowfeather had invited them to join him at the Grand Canyon in a few weeks. Since Lottie's surprise return, she'd granted the wishes of the press for a few interviews. They were interested both in her time with Elliot Teagartin, and in the new foundation she and her new spouse were forming. In one interview with Gil present, the two were asked how they'd met. Gil half-seriously answered, "We met when I kidnapped her," which the interviewer fortunately interpreted as a cute attempt at humor. Lottie and Gil were truly happy, and life seemed to be offering them a series of unceasing wonders. They felt themselves in a continuous state of amazement.

A few final notes of trivia – Lottie was getting some much-needed dental work done, and Gil was taking piano lessons.

The 747 cruised at high altitude over the Pacific Ocean, bound for Sydney, Australia, with a re-fueling layover in Honolulu. In the first-class compartment sat the usual assortment of affluent passengers, some traveling on business, some for pleasure. Unbeknownst to everyone on the plane, however, the most well-to-do individual on board was crammed into the economy section with the unfortunate less-than-wealthy travelers, undergoing the same 24 hour endurance test on this flight which had few, if any, vacant seats. Children chattered and skipped down the aisle, babies cried, and the more loud-mouthed of the passengers made their presence known, either through their typical bravado, or through the kinds of vulgar pretension that would drive everyone around them to distraction.

Keeping a low profile in such an atmosphere turned out to be a tall order, but our anti-hero felt up to the task. Twenty economy rows back from the entrance to the first-class section he sat in a dark-colored trench coat, sunglasses, and an expensive costume beard, which looked real enough. He was traveling under an assumed identity, and all of his fabulous wealth and influence had been insufficient to get him a seat in first class. Due to being in a hurry, and to his assumption that he'd have an easier time going unrecognized in the cheaper seats, he'd decided to settle for the only seat he could get, flying with the masses, and having to forego his usual luxury.

Having recently experienced a draught in the Northern American Wilderness with regard to his passion for spirits, Elliot Teagartin was making up for lost time. He was snarfing up all the low-brow scotch whiskey being offered by the flight attendants, and thereby easing the agitation of having to sit between a rotund man who snored without pause, and a pug-nosed woman who chattered away endlessly in pointless banter with a voice vaguely reminiscent of Ethel Merman.

Elliot had reached his breaking point in the Northern Wilderness, disbanding all of the remaining animals, with the exception of the horses, who escorted him relatively quickly to the nearest town. There, he got in touch with associates whom he felt he could trust to keep quiet, while making arrangements to pick him up and transport him to the nearest, soonest flight to the Australian Outback. Elliot had decided to enter what appeared to be a new frontier in a part of the world where he was less well known. He was looking forward to getting to know the kangaroos, koalas, and crocodiles, and, who knows? Perhaps he may even become friendly with the Aborigines.

Wherever he may go, and whatever may happen, Elliot felt confident that he would find new domains to conquer, exotic landscapes to subdue, and hungry gullible creatures to control. Deep within his troubled psyche lurked the belief that he was born to be a Master. The world around him was but mere clay on his potter's wheel.

The excitement was mounting in the sparkling new arena. A voracious audience, eager for the next new entertainment, packed the building. An official with the State Fire Marshall's Office stood in the wings, concerned that the legal limit had been exceeded, but his hands were tied. The powers that be had spoken, and the show would go on as planned. How selfish of him to think he should stand in the way of these people's enjoyment for the sake of something so mundane as public safety! The show's emcee stepped up to the microphone.

"Ladies and Gentlemen, the moment you've all been waiting for is upon us! Now, sit back, and float down a river of nostalgia, as we present to you this evening's entertainment, DANCING WITH THE MOOSE!" As the moose danced out onto the stage, the show's theme song began:

What would it take...
To come alive...
To turn your spirit loose...

The choreography was flawless. The moose swayed and swirled around each other in perfect precision, decked-out to the hilt in the grand Hollywood tradition.

You need not be...
A Lord or King...
Or fly like grebe or goose...

An orchestra composed of top-flight musicians played this exquisite waltz.

Put your cares away...
And seize the day...
You need not make excuse...

A chorus of singers stood by the orchestra, leading the audience in singing the theme song. Among the singers was a "newly-rehabilitated" ex-patient of a state institution for the mentally ill, Nicolai Zagorski.

On gilded wings...
Your spirit sings...
When you're dancing with the moose...

Ah, yes! The sweet smell of success. He'd toned down the act. Sanitized it. Made it acceptable for "prime time," and that turned out to be the ticket, the magic formula. Dancing with the Moose was just what the network needed to compete with the # 1 show on television, their rival network's smashing success, Original Sin. Balar hung from a chandelier in one of the lavish dressing rooms, smoking a cigar. He could tell that he had a hit on his hands, and he couldn't have been more pleased with himself. It would be nothing but "gravy" from here on out.

· 29 ·

Cale walked into George Cromwell's office after having returned from the Northern Wilderness. He sat down in one of the two chairs facing his boss's desk. George was on the phone, but looked intently at the young man he considered to be his "star reporter." Calen looked rather dejected and nervous.

"Listen, can I call you back? Yeah... yeah, let's do lunch. I'll meet you there at 12:30... yeah, thanks. Goodbye."

George called back to his secretary. "Could you hold my calls? Thank you." The wise editor continued to study the forlorn expression on Calen's face.

Before George could speak, Cale looked up at him and began his report. "I'm afraid I've come back empty-handed, George."

George had confidence in Cale, and was prepared to hear whatever he had to say.

"So... what happened?"

"We arrived at the spot where Teagartin had been ensconced for several weeks, but he wasn't there."

"Well, what was there?"

"There was plenty of evidence, but no Teagartin."

"Well, then you haven't exactly come back empty-handed,

have you? Tell me about the evidence."

"Wild animals in the general area that you could walk right up to without them getting spooked... strange spirit-like walls that seemed to delineate rooms in a kind of virtual building... camp appliances for cooking and washing clothes just left there... abandoned wagons... various odds and ends laying around. There were horse tracks leading back in the direction from which we came. We followed them back to Sunnyvale where the trail went cold. The guide estimated that he had the jump on us by about two or three days. He must have arrived in town sometime not long before we were leaving to look for him. From what we could see, it appeared that he just disbanded the rest of the animals and went to Sunnyvale on horseback. Where he went from there is anyone's guess..."

George was not displeased. He wanted solid reporting based on direct observation and experience, rather than dubious second-hand accounts, and he felt as if this was what he was getting from Cale, Teagartin, or no Teagartin. "Alright... look Cale, I know you're disappointed, but this is a start. Sooner or later, news about someone with his level of notoriety is bound to surface, and when it does, we'll jump on it. In the meantime, go ahead and write up what you found and get it to me. Like I said, I have a feeling this isn't over yet, not by a long shot."

Cale was somewhat heartened by George's encouraging words. "Okay, boss, I'll have it to you sometime tomorrow." He left George's office, walked back to his cubicle and sat down at his typewriter. Arthur Dinsmore jumped into his thoughts, and he began to speak to him quietly. "Artie, I hope you're listening to me right now... you're not forgotten... you're not forgotten... I promise you, I'll find that sonofabitch if it's the last thing I do..."

Sam and Father Dominic embraced. Sam's visit to the priest was drawing to a close. He was finishing his time at an

Orthodox Christian monastery in Arizona where Fr. Dominic was living, at least for the time being. His friend was like a new person - hopeful, luminescent, at peace. Sam's week at the monastery had been productive, involving a lot of time in prayer and contemplation. Though he had, over the past few months, reached clarity within himself as to who he was, what exactly to do about it hadn't been as clear. Along with the quiet time at the monastery, the Witness had visited him during the week, all of which lent focus to the direction he now felt called upon to take.

Sam had been like a student to the Witness since they'd met, and had received an education of sorts in navigating the finer levels of existence. Such experience had bequeathed him a sense of mission, a means of connecting with his ancestors and serving the will of the Great Spirit. After saying his goodbyes to Fr. Dominic, one of the monks drove Sam back to a nearby airstrip where he took off in his plane to meet Gil and Lottie at the airport in Flagstaff. The three were happy to be together again for the first time since Gil and Lottie's wedding. They sat at a restaurant in the airport complex and reminisced on their recent exploits in the Northern Wilderness. "What strikes me more than anything," Gil commented, "are the supernatural aspects of what we've been through. I used to pay lip service to mystical notions, but had never experienced them directly until recently. It had all been just a cerebral thing before, you know?"

"We were all in that dream together," Lottie responded. "You remember?"

"Yes!" said Sam. "That was a first for me too, to experience the same dream as others. I hadn't thought that was possible before..." The three compared notes on the dream, finding their accounts similar, before Sam continued. "But the thing that has captured my thoughts the most is the providence that seems evident in all of it. We've all gained a sense of purpose in our lives through these experiences. Now more than ever, I'm certain that nothing in life is coincidental, that everything happens according to a plan, a plan that is ultimately beneficial to us and others around us. The charitable organization you're starting seems to be a kind of fruit born of our endeavors, a kind of mission we've each been given to serve the greater good..."

The three flew in Sam's plane to the Grand Canyon, and spent the rest of the day together standing at its edge, peering down into the vast majestic crevice. This seemed a fitting end to their reunion, and as the time was drawing nigh for Gil and Lottie to catch a shuttle back to their hotel, Sam gave them each a hug. "I guess this is where we say goodbye. God bless you, my two friends."

"Take care, Sam," Gil responded.

Lottie smiled at Sam and felt tears welling up.

Sam began on the path toward his plane, and after going a ways, looked back at them again. "Hey... blonde woman and guy with a backpack, I'll see you in our dreams!"

They waved back at him and began to walk toward the shuttle, observing as he took flight in the distance. He flew directly above them and out over the canyon. Then Gil and Lottie stood spellbound as they watched Sam's plane disappear into a cloud and come out the other end as a resplendent eagle, lifting its wings gently up and down in a steady harmonious rhythm as it flew over the horizon and into the sunset.

"Did you see that??" Lottie remarked in astonishment.

Gil sighed. "Yes, I did... yes, I did..."

On the way to the hotel, Lottie broke the silence. "Do you think we'll really see Sam again?"

Gil thought for a moment. "You know, if he'd made that parting remark a few months ago, I'd have thought the idea preposterous. But now, I believe we will... I fully expect that we'll see Sam again in our dreams."

· epilogue ·

The Witness stood at the top of one of the oldest and tallest mountains in the Northern Wilderness. Gazing out over creation in limitless fashion, he looked into its breadth and depth and saw wondrous, joyous, virtuous, mundane, troublesome, sorrowful and evil things, and he smiled and shed tears. He considered the world of men, and its stewardship over the earth, and saw mixed results. The fortunate fact that such a wilderness still existed was a reflection of man's legacy to the future, as well as the unfortunate fact that a sizable percentage of the earth's natural resources had been extracted and squandered by the profit motive, and man's unquenchable appetite for the comfort, convenience and entertainments afforded by consumer goods.

Whatever the case may be, the Witness loved men, for they held within them the possibility of embracing nobility, and there were many souls left in the world who were reaching for the stars, despite the demons who'd continuously thrown their darts. As a servant of the Triune God, or the Great Spirit, as Sam Crowfeather referred to Him, the Witness never lost his faith in men, and dedicated himself tirelessly to their upliftment. Such an endeavor involved an unceasing struggle in which battles were won and lost, but the ultimate outcome of the war had yet to be determined.

He considered Sam, Anastasia, Lottie, Gil and Dominic to be among his victories thus far, but he knew that they'd need continued guidance and intervention in order to maintain a proper sense of perspective, and to avoid falling into prelest, or spiritual delusion. The Chosen One was a lesser creature than man, but a noble being nonetheless. His demise might be considered a loss by some, although a compelling reminder to men that the struggle itself has as much value as the outcome. The journalists Arthur, Calen, and George? Well, one was, and the other two are, caught up in the world of professional media. All of their heart and soul was, and is, consumed by this endeavor, and, to the degree that the media's aspiration is noble, their efforts might be edifying to others. If the aspiration is centered on decadence, then such men tend to get mired in the decadence. Arthur had the right idea, but unfortunately paid for his dangerous brand of free-lance journalism with his life.

Nicolai Zagorski's tortured existence was another complex mixture of loss and victory, driven by brain chemistry gone awry, and influenced by the degree to which he could humble himself enough to let go of his ambitions, and focus upon others, as well as accept guidance from others. His life would be a continual seesaw, but was not a hopeless, pointless, valueless existence plundered by the ravages of mental illness, as it may appear to some from the outside.

From the Witness's perspective, there was no life that wasn't worth living. Daddy Crump was a case in point. He was a loss, but not a total loss. He'd spent a considerable portion of his life medicating himself against the pain of losing his beloved wife. Though he'd often neglected his daughter, he truly loved her, and, in his own feeble manner, had imparted some positive values, which continue to play a part in her life to this day.

And then there was Elliot. The Witness felt as if he'd lost

the battle for Elliot long ago when the celebrated economist and philosopher was a child. A crucial attribute in the good health of the soul of any human being is humility, and the more famous and notorious Elliot became, his potential for gaining that most precious quality began to wane, until it was virtually non-existent. The spirit of Elliot Teagartin had been present in men since the first of them walked the earth, and the mother of all of Elliot's sour attributes was pride, the negative element that is the precursor to every fall. Elliot was among those who are often referred to as "the walking dead," though the Witness suspected that even regarding the walking dead there was still reason for hope. Miracles from the heavenly realms can be wrought, and perhaps when considering this possibility, there truly may not be such a phenomenon as those whose souls are presumed dead. After all, there isn't one among us who doesn't need a miracle, and human judgments are generally based on an abysmally incomplete understanding.

The Witness stood at the pinnacle of the mountain, while bulldozers and chainsaws were desecrating the forest below him at an alarming rate. But he was an optimist and an incurable romantic. He loved men and would continue loving them. Despite their irascible tendencies, they were given the potential to reach for, glimpse into, and for some, even to achieve union with, the Divine. The Witness would always be there for men, for they were eminently worthwhile creatures when their passions could be tamed, and their attention could be focused. He would remain committed to men, for he was driven by one primary impulse: compassion. He had come to love every part of them, even their weaknesses.

For they are but men and women, and they all fall short of perfection, even the saints among them. Why do they fall short? They get distracted, that's all...

They just get distracted.

AUTHOR'S BIOGRAPHY

Lou Stant has been a songwriter since 1972, and a professional musician/recording artist in Indiana since 1982. Having alternated since the early '80s between ensemble and solo work, he has been performing solo acoustic music since moving to Southern Indiana from Indianapolis in 1996, and is currently a part of a blues/jazz trio, "the Mizfits", which performs regularly in Brown and surrounding counties, and periodically in Indianapolis. "Alien Landscape" is Lou's sixth and most recent CD of original music. He also works as a Human Services Professional, is an ordained Eastern Orthodox Deacon, and is married with three children. Lou has been writing fiction since January of 2011, <u>Of Moose and Men</u> being the first of his completed works.